BETWEEN ISLANDS

Robert Coburn

Habent Sua Fata Libelli

ABSOLUTELY AMAZING eBOOKS

Manhanset House
Shelter Island Hts., New York 11965-0342

bricktower@aol.com • tech@absolutelyamazingebooks.com
• absolutelyamazingebooks.com

Library of Congress Cataloging-in-Publication Data
Coburn, Robert
Between Islands
p. cm.

1. FICTION / Mystery & Detective / Private Investigators. 2. FICTION / Thrillers / Crime. 3. FICTION / Thrillers / Suspense
Fiction, I. Title.
ISBN: 978-1-955036-66-5, Trade Paper

December 2023

BETWEEN ISLANDS

Robert Coburn

Other books by Robert Coburn

A Loose Knot

A Deadly Deception

The Pink Gun

Little Boxes

Bad Tidings

An Evil Number

Malice Murder

A Rage of Deaths

Dead Drop

Nails in the Coffin

Acknowledgments

Special thanks to Laura for her advice and editing. To my old publisher, Shirrel Rhoades at AbsolutelyAmazingEbooks. And to my new publisher, John T. Colby Jr., at Brick Tower Press.

Chapter 1

In the trailing edge of night, a gloomy curtain had been drawn over the town of Hilo on the island of Hawaii, a presage to the approaching storm.

Had it thundered the old man might've been startled awake and lived. But the clouds had held their tongues. And his weakened heart had tarried too long between beats and now the irreversible chemistry of death had been set into motion.

He stopped breathing and silently sank into eternity.

The wind picked up and sheets of chilling rain began to sweep across the harbor's breakwater and spit angrily against the windows of buildings and homes, some long deprived of any tropical charm.

Suddenly, a barrage of thunder fell with such impact that children asleep in their beds cried out fearfully and lights were turned on in many houses.

The woman sat up, wondering how her husband lying next to her could sleep through all of this.

~~~

In Honolulu, two hundred and ten miles away, Detective Joe Cheo's eyes fluttered open. Something apparently had disturbed him. Hearing nothing more, he decided it was probably just a dream. Though whatever it was had now given him an inexplicable feeling. An unsettling chill passed over him.

He took a couple of deep breaths to clear his head and looked over to see the bedside clock. It read four fifteen a.m. Two hours before he had to get up.

He muttered something unintelligible and settled back onto the mattress but sleep was not to return. Half an hour later and fully awake, he resignedly slid out of bed and went to take a shower.

Now dressed in slacks and an aloha shirt, he stepped out onto the balcony of his tiny studio apartment in a building on Ala Mona Boulevard. The sun still hunkered below the horizon but the brightening eastern sky promised another lovely day. He could hear the surf at Waikiki. He imagined there'd already be some die-hard surfers lining up for the incoming sets. He envied them and might've joined in himself had he had the day off but this morning's mysterious early wakeup offered another and perhaps more pertinent opportunity. To walk his old beat.

District 1 which comprised downtown Honolulu and Chinatown was in the midst of the swing shift, the night crew of characters and usual habitats exchanging haunts with the day crew. This had always been a good time for Joe to mingle with the masses and put names on faces.

He'd worked all shifts on patrol as a uniformed officer in several districts for seven years after joining the Honolulu Police Department, spending the last three years in District 1. Standing a little over six feet, he was taller than the average Hawaiian and presented an impressionable image on the street. He'd also earned a reputation for being a fair cop and one who was never disrespectful to anyone, all of which went a long way toward gaining trust. And which in turn had always provided him with more than a little insight as to what was going on. On one occasion, he was able to point out to a homicide detective a suspect he'd recognized on his beat.

Even though he was now with detectives and in plain clothes, he never missed a chance to touch bases with the old crowd. He set out to make the rounds before going to the station.

~~~

"Get somebody over here right now," Albert Cheo demanded. "Twenty four Noalani Lane. It's right by the Wailuku River past the park. Write that down."

He was on the phone with the 911 operator.

"No, he's unconscious," he said, looking at his sister-in-law with concern. "How would I know for how long? His wife discovered him that way this morning. His name? I told you that, for God's sake. George Cheo and, yes, he's my brother. Please, no more questions. Just send an ambulance. Of course, I realize you have to notify the police. Stop stalling and get on with it. What? Hello?"

The phone went dead. He hung it up.

"Must be a line down from the storm," he grumbled. "Those people are maddening. All I can say is I'd better be hearing a siren blowing soon."

Albert lived in an ohana, which is a small separate home from the main house on the same property. Ohana means family in the Hawaiian language. It is an old idea for keeping families together.

His father had originally built it for his own aging parents, the main house having become too crowded by the growing family. After they'd passed on, the expectation was that he and his wife would eventually move in and so it would continue on down the line with the next generation. Until then, however, the little home could be a hideout for the boys to play in and an occasional retreat for the parents. But their father's death from a heart attack, who had become an early widower, his wife having died in an accident, put that plan on hold and left the ohana unoccupied again. George had gotten engaged and once he was married the expectation was there'd be lots of children coming. Albert suggested that his brother take the main house and he would live in the small obana.

Helen Cheo had run out there to get him when she'd been unable to awaken her husband earlier that morning.

"This is so terrible," she fretted. "I don't know what to do, Albert. I should have tried to get him up when the storm awoke me. You do believe he'll be all right, don't you?"

"Let's just wait for the ambulance," Albert said and patted her hand.

He'd known from the moment he'd seen his brother lying in bed that there was nothing anyone could do. The body had begun to grow cold. Still, he'd thought it best not to alarm Helen any further. She was holding up pretty well, as it were. He'd soon have more than enough on his hands.

"Would you like some coffee, Albert?" Helen asked, turning toward the kitchen. "I can make a pot. It'd give me something to do."

"Nothing right now, Helen. Just sit down and try to relax. Help will be here soon."

"Do you think we should call Joe?" Helen asked anxiously.

"Not this moment," Albert said patiently. "Later after things have settled down and we know more."

The telephone rang. Apparently the downed line had been repaired.

~~~

"Good morning, Samuel," Billy Bahia, the bartender at the Bamboo Hut, greeted a man standing in the doorway. "I'm not open yet."

The Bamboo Hut was down a side street off of the main drag at the Hilo harbor. Tourists might call it quaint but in truth it was simply a nondescript rundown joint that'd been there forever and catered mostly to a mix of locals. There was no problem getting your butt kicked here but if you watched your mouth and kept your eyes off someone's girlfriend or wife, you could get a decent drink and spend some passable time enjoying the neighborhood gossip.

"Heard the music playing," Samuel said. "Thought you were open so I could grab a beer before work. Got a lot of cleaning up to do after that damn storm. Also, it's my granddaughter's birthday. Can't miss that."

"Yeah, water was everywhere," Billy agreed. "'Bout got it mopped up. Turned on the jukebox for company. Say happy birthday for me to your granddaughter."

Billy rattled out a beer from the cooler and put it on the bar.

"What the hell, bro, let's celebrate that birthday," he said. "As of this moment we're unofficially open."

He uncapped a bottle for himself.

"Thanks," Samuel said, slapping down a couple dollars on the bar. "Be just this one. Don't want to be late."

"It's on the house," Billy said, pushing back the money. "Got some big news this morning. George Cheo checked out for the big island in the sky."

"What?"

"Heard it on my police scanner," Billy said, indicating the device nestled on a shelf behind him. "One down, one more to go. Never did care for any of them. Joe, the kid, was okay. He got smart and moved the hell out before too much of that Cheo shit rubbed off on him."

"I don't know what to say," Samuel said. "Hell, I didn't even know George was sick."

"Well, he ain't sick no more," Billy laughed. "Dying ends that."

"Used to see both of them in here," Samuel said. "George and Albert. That was some time back, though. Things were different then."

"Ain't they always," Billy agreed. "I'd just starting working here. Albert would drop by to collect the monthly shakedown for that Samoan gang that was running things then. Late on a payment with that bunch and you might get your place dismantled one night. Albert thought he was a big shot but he was just a glorified bagman. George would tag along with him and tell war stores. He liked the songs on the jukebox. Said they reminded him of the time back in Honolulu. He also liked to have a drink or three on the house."

"Well, he did have a ringside seat at Pearl Harbor," Samuel said. "I kind of enjoyed that particular story."

"Yeah, that one would spill out after the third drink," Billy laughed. "Wonder what it was really like?"

* * *

Neon signs colored the sidewalks as ribbons of bobbing white hats on sailors flowed from one bar to the next. The fleet was in and the future of young men in love never offered more promise than a tropical night.

George Cheo had come to Honolulu to visit his childhood friend, Tommy Kitagawa, and help him celebrate his recent birthday. They were both the same age and were born a month apart to the day.

Tommy's dad, Hiedi, was an Issei, a first generation Japanese, and had gotten occasional work at the Cheo family's construction company which George's grandfather had founded in Hilo and now his dad ran.

Nearly half the population of Hawaii had Japanese ties. Most immigrants labored in the fields for little pay but Hiedi was lucky, he had carpentry skills. Not that the Cheos paid him all that much.

Hiedi had met young George at the construction sites. His dad often brought him there after school to learn something about that part of the business since he would be next in line to take it over. Hiedi recognized that this was an opportunity to teach his son some of his trade and suggested that George might like a classmate. George's dad went along with the idea.

Tommy and his dad spoke to each other in Japanese. George discovered that he had an ear for the language. Soon he'd become reasonably fluent himself.

When Tommy was old enough, he also went to work for the construction firm alongside of his dad.

Recently the construction work had slackened in Hilo and Hiedi and Tommy had temporary moved to Honolulu where a big government project was underway at Hickam Field, the U.S. Army airbase. There was money to be made.

Between Islands

The two friends had done the town celebrating but had called it an early night and had gone back to the tiny apartment where Tommy and his dad lived. They'd needed to be at the airfield by six a.m. the next day. Though it would be Sunday and they'd would've liked to have had the day off, the overtime money was too good to miss.

George had been given the sofa for the night since he was a guest. That was usually Tommy's bed but he'd slept on a tatami mat in the bedroom with his father. They'd be up and gone by dawn.

George had awakened a little before eight the next morning. He lay flat on his back staring at the ceiling fan, a lazy carousel mixing the perfume of night jasmine and garden flowers warming in the morning sun.

He propped himself up and looked out the window toward Pearl Harbor. The sheets felt cool and sexy on his naked body.

Along battleship row he could count the capital ships-of-war moored bow to stern and port to starboard. He recognized the Arizona. Smoke and steam wafted from her stacks. The entire scene was an impressive painting of power framed by the window of his bedroom.

Flying low through Kolekole Pass, Flight Sergeant Tochigi Ameniya saw Schofield Barracks come into view and pass quickly beneath the wings of his torpedo bomber. Smoke from bomb blasts ahead whisked by the cockpit. Soldiers scattered like ants running across the open parade fields. Some of them were firing small arms, rifles and pistols, at the attacking airplanes.

Ameniya pushed the control stick forward and the airplane entered a shallow dive. The engine whined as his airspeed increased. Gray ships filled his windshield and gun muzzles spewed orange flames at him as he leveled off barely feet above the water. He released his torpedo and pulled back on the stick. The airplane, free of its deadly weight, zoomed straight up into the black and fiery sky.

Like swarming green dragon flies with orange suns on their wings, the airplanes dove again and again through the haze of gunfire and bursting shells. The helpless ships rode low in the water, some listing drunkenly to port or starboard. The fires burned recklessly and explosions were everywhere.

George Cheo sat motionless in bed. His eyes widened as the Arizona, burning fiercely, suddenly blew a huge plume of smoke from her stacks and seemed to levitate inches above the water before toppling over to vanish in a horrific release of energy.

An errant projectile, having missed its mark, continued on course directly for the house where George was witnessing the destruction of the Pacific Fleet. Suddenly, the end of the world happened.

"How do you feel?" a strange voice inquired,

George was afraid to answer. He held his eyes shut.

"Do you speak English?"

George opened his eyes.

He saw that he was in a bed and a man dressed in a military uniform stood next to it.

"Where am I?" he asked. "Who are you?"

"I am a United States Army officer. You are in a hospital. And we need to know who you are."

"I'm George Cheo. I live in Hilo."

"You were found sitting in the street naked and delirious in front of a building that had been bombed. You were speaking Japanese. That concerns us."

"I learned it as kid from our neighbors," George explained. "I was visiting my friend here. What's the difference anyway? Lots of people speak Japanese. I'm getting out of here. I need to go home."

The officer looked coldly at George and then turned to the military policeman standing next to him.

"Sergeant, take this man into custody," he ordered.

* * *

"Lucky they didn't shoot him on the spot when they thought he was a spy," Samuel said. "Instead they made him an interpreter."

"Pearl Harbor might've been the only time George saw any real action," Billy chuckled. "I heard the interpreters were kept behind the lines."

"Safest place to be, if you ask me," Samuel said. "Still, there were some terrible things you had to have seen no matter where you were. Can't say how that might affect you."

"Well, he could be a real prick sometimes," Billy said. "Don't know if the war had anything to do with that. Probably born that way. Runs in the family. War could've fucked him up more, though."

"I'd seen that in other vets. Might've been what cost him the sheriff's job.." Samuel said. "Though he wasn't much of a sheriff anyway, so it was no big loss."

"He only got the job because old man Cheo had some political pull," Billy said. "Passed him off as a war hero. Ain't that a laugh."

~ ~ ~

"Who was that who called awhile ago, Albert?" Helen asked. "I must have drifted off."

"Just another person saying how sorry they are. Word must be out."

"I thought it might have been Mrs. Hamakua," Helen said. "She lives a few streets down."

"I know where Mrs. Hamakua lives," Albert replied. "Also I expect she'll be here sooner or later to pay her respects. Along with half the town."

"It's pretty outside," Helen stated. "Look, Albert, the sun's trying to come out."

She pulled back the sheer window curtains in the breakfast nook where she sat to reveal a carefully tended flower garden. The colors ran together on the wet glass panes.

Dr. Kimo Yeung, who was the family physician and also the county medical examiner, stepped into the kitchen.

"Excuse me," he said, "Could I speak with you for a minute, Albert? In private."

Albert led him into the living room.

"The state could require an autopsy," Yeung told him. "It's a normal procedure with all deaths. Even though there's nothing suspicious about George's passing they could still want one. I can have it done here at Hilo Medical Center."

"An autopsy?" Albert questioned. "Why? He had a bad heart. You treated him for it. You just said there was nothing suspicious."

"Yes, I know. His heart had grown extremely weak since the attack. I was hoping there'd be some improvement. In fact, I almost thought for a while there might have been a little. Still, I wasn't surprised that it finally gave out. Shame, though, he wasn't all that old. And you should come in for an examination. It's been far too long, Albert. That little murmur you have shouldn't be forgotten, I might add."

"We're not talking about me, doctor," Albert said. "We're talking about my brother. And I'm feeling fine, I might also add."

"If you're concerned about delaying any funeral plans, I can perhaps expedite the autopsy order," Yeung said.

"You think I'm going to let a stranger cut up my brother?" Albert snapped.

"I sympathize with your feelings," Yeung said. "But I still have to write a report as the county medical examiner. That's part of the procedure in any death, as I tried to explain."

"I don't care about any procedure," Albert said angrily. "Stuff your goddamn procedure. No autopsy. George gave me power-of-attorney a while back. So that's the way it's going to be. No damn autopsy."

"That decision is neither yours nor mine to make," Yeung told him firmly. "It belongs to the state. Has nothing to do with power-of-attorney. I'm sorry about George but that's just the way it is."

Albert glared at Yeung. In an earlier time the little man wouldn't have dared to speak to him like that.

"Write your damn report then," he said brusquely.

"Thank you. As I explained, there's not anything unusual about your brother's death. So I won't recommend any further examination and the state will probably go along with that. I'll get the report in today. Should hear back tomorrow. Meanwhile, you can make arrangements for the funeral. The body will remain at the hospital."

"He has a name," Hellen said softly.

She had entered unknowably entered the room.

"I beg your pardon?" Yeung said, turning to her.

"The body you mentioned," Helen smiled. "His name is George Cheo. He was my husband."

"I didn't mean to be disrespectful, Mrs. Cheo," Yeung apologized. "I'll be leaving now. Thank you, I can see my way out."

Nothing more was said until he'd gone.

"I think Roberts Funeral Home can handle every thing for us, Helen," Albert said. "Maybe something traditional."

He picked up a calabash bowl made of Koa wood and then set it back on the shelf containing more of them in different sizes. Koa was the wood of the royals and today a single calabash from that era can run into the thousands. His grandfather had collected them long ago. Other than their being very old, no one had ever traced the lineage.

Chapter 2

"Good morning, Detective Cheo," Lola Kahamena said. "Glad you could make it in before everyone went home for the day."

She was the detectives secretary. The position was a luxury not shared in all districts. It wouldn't be wise for anyone to contest it, however. Lola had friends and had been around for awhile.

"Running a little late this morning, Lola," Joe said. "Had a couple of stops that delayed me. Hope I didn't miss anything."

One stop had included a drive across town to the Sunrise Cafe for a leisurely breakfast and a couple of cups of Kona coffee.

"Actually, you had a telephone call. Some person named Ricky Ricola. Said he needed to talk with you. I hope you have the number. He hung up before I could ask."

Wow, he hadn't heard that name since forever, Joe thought. Wonder what his old snitch is up to?

Ricola was a petty thief Joe had arrested on several occasions during the time he'd worked patrol. He wasn't a violent person. Just had a penchant for taking things that didn't belong to him. Nothing big, mostly shoplifting. He'd given Ricky a break now and then, depending on the circumstances. Joe had considered it an investment. Ricky had felt beholden to him and was always good for street information.

"How long ago did he call?" Joe asked.

"An hour or so. He sounded kind of fidgety."

Fidgety was the perfect word to describe Ricky, Joe thought.

"Don't forget to sign in," Lola reminded.

The department lieutenant had recently installed a chalkboard for all detectives to sign in and out. Everyone hated it.

At his desk, Joe flipped through his phone book to Ricky's number and dialed. He pictured the pay phone ringing in the dingy hallway at the rundown apartment building where Ricky lived.

"Yeah?" a weary voice answered.

"I'm Detective Joe Cheo with the HPD. Wondering if…"

"Christ almighty, are you guys ever gonna finish bugging me?" the voice interrupted. "I already told you all I know. Frank Lofume rented here. Always paid on time. That's all that matters to me. What else anyone does is his own business. I keep my nose out of it. Okay?"

This was weird, Joe thought. What was he talking about?

"May I ask who you are, sir?"

"My name is Tony Boyd. I'm the building superintendent. Also, the maintenance man, plumber, electrician, whatever you've got. In other words, I run this broken down flophouse. All right, let's have it then. What do you need?"

"I'm trying to get in touch with Ricky Ricola. Does he still live there? This is an old telephone number I have and I wasn't sure."

"You got the right number, detective. It's a pay phone, if you didn't already know. Our apartments don't have any la-de-dah private phones. I just happened to be here when it rang so I picked up. That's the house rule. Phone rings and you're near it, answer the damn thing. Yeah, the cops been around all morning about Frank Lofume. Thought that's who you were calling about. Okay, Ricky Ricola lives here but I saw him leave awhile ago. Hasn't come back. And to save you time, I don't know any more about him that I do about Lofume. "

This guy is some character, Joe thought.

"When you see Ricky next, please tell him to call me," he said. "Detective Joe Cheo. Itd be a big help and I'd appreciate it."

The man hung up without another word.

Joe leaned back in his chair and unconsciously fingered the scar on his left cheek. This was interesting, he thought. Who was Frank Lofume? What happened? Why were the police there? Did this have anything to do with why Ricky had called him?

Detective Walt Douglas plopped down in his chair. He'd been working on one of the department's computers.

Douglas worked burglary and his desk faced Joe's. The two of them had partnered on a few cases before Joe had been relegated to investigating auto theft, which was low man in the detective lineup.

"Damn department computer," he complained. "I'll never get onto these things. You any good with them, Joe?"

"Yeah, actually I am," Joe said. "It's not rocket science, just takes a little practice. You know, someday you'll probably have a computer right there on your desk. Modern times, man. Get with the program."

"That's what they said about two-way-radio wristwatches," Walt joked. "I'm still waiting for mine."

""Dick Tracy fan, huh? Didn't realize you were that old, Walt. Computers will get easier, believe me. Look how far cellphones have come since they first came out."

"Yeah, right, the things are still like carrying a walkie-talkie. Well, I gotta run. Talk with the victim again in a burglary case. I haven't even had time to read the paper. You can have it. See you around."

Walt left the room and Joe reached across the desk for the newspaper. The lead story concerned the heating up of the war in Iraq. Another story reported on President Ronald Reagan's meeting with Margaret Thatcher. Feature piece on the last princess of Hawaii, who also happens to raise quarter horses. One of the animals bred on her mainland farm recently won a race. Joe scanned that with little interest and turned to the next page where his eyes fell on a small article about a body having been discovered in a parking lot at Pearl Harbor last night. Police are viewing it as a suspicious death. The victim was identified as Frank Lofume of Honolulu.

Joe put down the paper. What an amazing coincidence, he thought.

~~~

"Tell me again, Tiny," Albert said tightly. "Try not to leave out anything."

Tiny was a hanger-on from an old Samoan criminal gang that had once controlled the islands but no longer existed. He now worked for Albert doing odd jobs. He had been a large and powerful man when he first acquired the nickname during the gang's heyday. It became the only name he went by. Even to this day. He wasn't somebody you would mess with back then but age had exacted a heavy price over the years. They sat in the small living room of the ohana.

"Like I said, everything went without a hitch," Tiny began, then seemingly confused about what next to say, paused.

"Take all the time you need," Albert interjected.

He had long known that Tiny became flustered when rushed.

"Let's start from when you got to the airport," he suggested. "That might be better anyway. Go through everything in order. You okay now?"

Tiny took in a breath and nodded.

"I rented the van and drove to the docks to pick up Frank," he said. "He was waiting where the barge and tug had tied up. It'd gotten there on time from Maui."

"How long has Frank been with us?" Albert asked, diverting momentarily. "I forget."

"Almost a year," Tiny said. "He knew Hugo and Pepe Tanaka. Lived not far from them in Honolulu. Worked on the docks. Had his seaman's papers, too. Started doing some special favors for them.

Keeping an eye out on what was coming in and letting them know where it was being warehoused. Pepe recommended he come work for us after Hugo had that accident and he was shutting down their business there. Frank's been okay."

"Hugo was a good man," Albert said ruefully. "Sorry to have lost him. But what can you do? Those things happen. Go on. You've picked up Frank. Now what?"

"Then we drove out to the warehouse," Tiny continued. "The drugs were packed in a crate with some dishes. Wasn't a big crate. Like something somebody was sending home. I cut open one bag and tested it. It was primo. I gave them the money. Everybody was happy. I was glad I had Frank with me. I wasn't expecting trouble but I didn't know those people. But nothing happened. We loaded the crate in the van and left."

"There was seventy-five thousand dollars in that briefcase you gave them," Albert said bitterly. "Do you realize how much money that is?"

Tiny looked at the floor.

"Never mind," Albert said. "So the two of you went straight back to the docks from the warehouse, no stopping off for a beer or anything."

"No, sir," Tiny said emphatically. "Not anywhere. Straight back."

"Okay, what next?"

"Frank and me put the crate on the tug where nobody would mess with it. He was going to be off work for the next couple of days. I didn't know that till then but I figured it was all right. Union had already sent a replacement. The barge was set to leave on time."

"Unions take care of their friends," Albert noted. "I've always given preference to union men when it's possible. Now the crate's on the tug and you're ready to return to here. What next?"

"That's right. Frank said he didn't need a ride home. Said he was going to hang around for awhile, so I drove to the airport and turned in the van and caught my flight back here. I told you all this before, Albert."

"I realize that, Tiny. I just want to go through the entire process from start to finish again. It's important in case we've missed something. Now, the barge has arrived here on schedule. Go ahead."

"I went down to the dock. The barge was already there with the tug. Must've been a rough ride through that storm. Crate was right where we'd put it on the tug. Opened it. Only the dishes inside."

Albert got up and walked over to the window.

"You should've come with it," he grumbled. "Especially since Frank wouldn't be there. That was a mistake."

"But I had a ticket to fly back," Tiny said.

Albert shot him a look.

"So what could have happened?" he asked, ignoring Tiny's reasoning. "That was pure heroin. You could cut that twenty times, more even, and still have a product better than anything else available right now. You're looking at several million dollars at street value. I can't afford that kind of loss at the moment. There are things in the works you don't know about, Tiny. But I can tell you this much. There's a lot of money to make if you're smart enough to get in at the beginning. This loss is a personal embarrassment. It was difficult enough to arrange the buy. And don't think this screwup will go unnoticed. I want to know who's responsible. And I want those drugs back."

Albert turned and looked straight at Tiny, who'd begun to perspire.

"It had to be somebody on the tug," Tiny said, swiping at his brow. "One of the crew. Maybe that union replacement. Somehow knew about the drugs and stole them."

Albert fixed him with a suspicious eye and waited for a full minute before speaking.

"Find out who's behind this, Tiny," he said quietly. "Get that person's name. I'm depending on you. Don't disappoint me."

The two men headed back to the main house. Abraham Kaneoe met them coming up the walk.

"Abe, good to see you," Albert greeted . "Guess you know about George."

"Word gets out quick," Abe said. "How are you doing and how is Helen?"

"We're doing as well as can be expected, Abe," Albert said, holding the front door open. "Come on in. Looks like it's going to start raining again."

Abe turned sideways to get through the doorway and past Albert. He was an enormous man and one of the few full-blooded Hawaiians left in the islands. He and George had known each other since childhood.

"Abe Kaneoe is here, Helen," Albert called out. "We're in the living room."

Hellen entered the room and Abe embraced her with a smothering hug.

"Have a seat, Abe," she said, once released. "I've got some fresh coffee on the stove."

"I'm all right, Helen," he said, sinking into an overstuffed chair. "Don't bother about me. Albert, do you remember the time George and I saw the ula lele?"

"That's a disembodied spirit, Helen," Albert explained.

Helen gave him a quick look.

Stories, even funny ones about the deceased, are traditionally told as a show of affection for the family members. They are part of a celebration of the deceased's life that begins at the time of death and continues on through the funeral.

"I certainly do remember, Abe," Albert said. "Why don't you share that again with us?"

"Well, we'd gone out hunting early that morning," Abe began. "It was a fine day to shoot a wild pig. We'd ridden all the way over to near the Kona side and were going through some thick bushes when I spied something move. I whispered to George.

* * *

"Pssst! George, think there's a pig in that brush over there. You see him?"

George nodded that he did and slid his Winchester 30/30 out from its case strapped to the saddle. The heft of the rifle felt comfortable. His hands warmed to the smooth old walnut wood of the stock, its grip checkering worn over the years. Abe also removed his rifle.

Both men silently dismounted, dropping the horse's reins to the ground.

George carefully cocked the hammer back on the Winchester.

Fifty feet away, the boar had now frozen absolutely still in the shadows of the scrub brush. Its whole being focused on the familiar and loathsome smell of horses and men. But the breeze had given up and there was nothing to point a direction to the danger he sensed.

Years ago, the smell of horses and men had set his instincts for survival into flight. But the horses had drawn down upon him and the strong rope had quickly brought him to ground. He'd fought wildly but the men had held him fast and with a slash of the buck knife he'd been castrated and the top of his right ear lopped off.

Turning a pig into a eunuch makes them grow fatter. Hunters sometimes capture a small boar, castrate it and mark its ear with a cut. Over time, a seventy-five pound fixed porker might grow into a tasty hundred and twenty-five pound slab of bacon.

Once the men had released him, he'd scrambled into the protection of the thick brush. Then against every nerve imploring him to continue running, he'd stopped short and waited until the scent of horses and men was gone and only the sun-warmed smell of lava rock and brush remained. It was then that he knew he was safe.

Now they had returned and he waited again but not as the same pig.

"Did you see his ear?" Abe hissed to George. "Sonofabitch must weigh close to two-fifty."

"Wonder why he hasn't been picked him off?" George mused.

"Could be nobody's hunted this side of the island for a long time," Abe said. "That or he's too smart."

"I'll slip around behind him," George said.

"No, I might shoot you," Abe said, placing a hand on his shoulder.

They crouched and moved closer to the brush.

"He's probably on the other side of that big lava rock," George whispered and raised his rifle.

The lava rock suddenly exploded.

With a snapping of twigs and angry snorts, the boar catapulted from the brush directly at the two men. One of his tusks ripped through Abe's pants leg flinging him into George and knocking him down. The Winchester rifle spun away to disappear down a deep crevice where the hammer struck to fire its last shot ever to be heard.

The horses had seen enough and bolted full-hoof for home.

"What the hell was that?" George asked, getting to his feet.

"Must've been some kind of ula lele," Abe said, sitting up. "Where are the horses?"

"Where's my gun?" George said looking around.

The walk home would have been more pleasant if it hadn't taken all night.

* * *

"George never did find that rifle of his," Abe said. "I went back a couple of time myself to look for it. I believe Madame Pele has it on the mantle over her fireplace now. What do you think of that story, Helen? George and me, we sure had some good times together back then."

"Thank you, Abe," Helen said. "Sure I can't get you some coffee?"

"No, thanks. I've got to be running. Have you made plans for the funeral? I know it's early yet but people are asking."

"Roberts will be handling everything," Albert said. "Thinking having something here at the house. A traditional funeral."

"George would like that," Abe smiled.

Chapter 3

Joe walked down the small hallway off the detectives room to a set of stairs that led to the roof. He often went up there when he needed a place to think without being disturbed.

He stepped outside and looked across the harbor. He could see the Arizona Memorial in the distance. Many commercial vessels were now docked along the piers that were once battleship row.

His father had taken him to the memorial when he was a child and the family had gone to Honolulu. An outing he'd treasured ever since because he'd rarely gone anywhere with just his dad. He remembered him silently reading the names of the men who'd died that day etched in a marble wall inside the memorial with only his lips moving. Afterwards, while they waited on the platform for the boat to take them back to shore, he'd watched tiny circles spreading out in rainbow colors on the water's surface as oil continued to seep from the bunkers in the sunken ship. He had imagined the sailors still down there. Nine hundred in total.

At the moment, however, his attention was being given to the earlier phone call from Ricky Ricola and the newspaper article he'd just read about a suspicious death at the waterfront. Then there had been Ricky sounding jittery when he'd called. Both he and the victim living at the same address. Was there a connection? He was almost of a mind to pay the building superintendent a visit. However, it would be better to hold off on that for the time being. Sticking his nose into someone else's investigation at another station probably wouldn't be appreciated. Still, it ate at him.

He went back downstairs to the detectives' room.

~~~

Ricky Ricola had taken the bus to Pearl Harbor. It'd been a forty-minute ride along the route from the bus stop nearest his apartment and he'd nervously stared out the window the entire time.

He didn't know what he had expected to see but to his relief nothing that he might've thought threatening had shown up and now he was seated at the bar and feeling a little easier. It was still early and only a couple other customers were in the place. A few hours later and it would be packed.

Ricky fingered the key in his pocket. It fitted a locker in the back room. The lockers were mostly rented to military personnel. Mainly to those who lived on base and needed some extra storage space.

He had recently rented a couple of the lockers there himself for Frank Lofume and Frank had paid him three hundred dollars to do that and the other thing with a promise of more to come. Easiest money he'd ever made and now considering what had happened was also probably the dumbest thing he'd ever done in his life.

But this time he was going to do something smart. He finished his beer and went to the locker room.

~~~

Everybody must start cooking when they hear someone has died. Or so it would appear judging from the covered bowls and lidded pots placed on every surface in the kitchen. It was still early afternoon.

"How will we ever eat all of this food?" Helen asked herself.

"Just put it in the freezer for later, Helen," Lucy Amito, one of her neighbors who'd just walked in, told her.

"There's just so much to do, Lucy," Hellen said. "I don't know how we're going to get through this."

Several other women, all neighbors, stood quietly chatting in the large living room, which could almost be mistaken for a museum. Photographs of Hawaii taken from an earlier time and heavily framed in veneered wood competed for attention on the walls. Other antiquities occupied the corners.

"Helen," one of the women called. "Come and tell us how you met George. That's such a wonderful story. Do you mind?"

"Oh, you don't want to hear that old thing," Helen said, blushing and coming into the room. "Besides, it would give away my age."

"Don't be silly, dear. Of course we would love to hear it. And don't worry about the other. Half of us here are older than you. The other half just won't admit it."

"Well, all right then," Helen smiled and sat on a leather hassock.

"It was an absolutely stunning day in Hilo," she began. "I had gone to work early at the children's school to take my class on a field trip to the tidal pools. Mrs. Eans had started that outing before she retired and I took over her class. She was probably doing it while I was still living in Kauaii. Well, enough of that. When we got to the beach, the sea was so calm that it was all I could do to keep the children from running straight into the water."

She paused for a moment as the memories formed in a tragic train of thought.

"You could see bright flashes of color in the little holes and lava pockets as the tiny fish flitted around in them," she continued. "The children were delighted. Then an amazing thing happened. The water began to recede."

* * *

A few children noticed at first and soon everyone had grown silent in wonder. Deeper pools formed, flopping with fish, as the tide raced out to sea.

Beyond the horizon, a wall of ocean began to rise above the quarreling swells. Seismographs in Oakland, California, had recorded the undersea event at eight-point-two on the Richter Scale.

Still several miles away out at sea, the tsunami raced toward land and rose like a distant mountain range as it passed over the up-sloping bottom. The enormous draught of the giant wave pulled water from the shore as it closed on the island.

Helen stood spellbound as the fantastic spectacle became more wondrous by the second. Then she grew pale at the reality that was about to befall. She screamed at the children.

"Come! Come! "

But they were having too much fun to hear. The wave bore down with all of its mass. Its present course would take the main body of water to the south. The suddenness of the swelling tide, however, ushered in a destruction all of its own.

"Everybody grab hands and run to the beach!"

The children did as they were told but the tiny chain began to break and some stumbled and fell.

Where the ocean bottom's secrets had been exposed seconds before, they were instantly hidden again by the massive inrushing tide. Fish finned through the roiling waters as the ocean retook the sandy beach.

Surf crashed over Helen. Turbulent currents pulled at her feet like strong hands and dragged her back toward the depths. She surfaced to see debris bobbing around her.

"Oh, blessed Jesus, don't let me die!" she cried.

As the waves towered above her, a wooden door popped out of one. She swam to it and, with the last of her strength, pulled herself up and on.

Rescue parties had formed quickly and were scouring the beach area.

George Cheo stroked a paddle with four other men in a long canoe. There was no talk, only the sound of the blades cutting through the water. As the waves lifted them, George craned his neck to search. There among the floating pieces of broken lumber, bottles and dead seabirds he saw Helen hanging onto her door.

Sadly, one child who had been with her was lost. A little boy.

* * *

"And that's how I met my husband," she said, her voice softening almost to a whisper.

"That's such a lovely story," Lucy beamed. "And later you both were blessed with a wonderful child."

"Joe was indeed a gift," Helen replied with a smile.

Chapter 4

Busywork had kept Joe occupied while the afternoon inched along. He was getting ready to leave for the day when his phone rang.

"This is Detective Cheo," he answered.

"Hello, detective, I was just thinking of you."

Joe grinned.

"Hi, Lillian," he said. "Good things or bad things?"

"Bad things can be good things," she laughed. "You ought to know that by now."

Lillian was his wife. They'd originally met at Schofield Barracks on Oahu. Her dad had introduced them.

Joe had been seriously wounded in Viet Nam toward the end of his tour and was assigned to light duty in a replacement company at Schofield while he completed his enlistment. Lillian's dad, Master Sergeant William Collins, was the top sergeant in the unit, which was being prepared for deployment. Coincidentally, Joe and he had originally met at Aha Trang in Viet Nam where Joe had been sent for special training and their paths had crossed once again at an undisclosed location in the Central Highlands while Joe was a member of a long-range recon patrol unit.

Lillian and her mom had come to the base to see a parade. She was an only child and had been an Army brat all of her life. There'd been some kind of a spark between her and Joe at that first meeting and they'd sporadically kept in touch but that was about it.

Her father had been reassigned soon afterwards and he and her mom had left Hawaii. Lillian had taken that as an opportunity to get out on her own. She'd stayed behind and had gotten a job with an interior design group in Honolulu.

Joe had kicked around in Hilo for awhile after being discharged from the Army, deciding what he wanted to do next. He could return to college. He had completed his freshman year and was two semesters into the next year when he'd decided on the spur of the moment to join the Army. He'd long ago dismissed any idea of joining the family business, despite his uncle's pressure. His dad had been indifferent, which was his usual stance on just about anything. Finally, and instead of remaining in Hilo and going back to school, he joined the Honolulu police department. It wasn't that he'd always had an interest in police work. And one wouldn't have been wrong in thinking so since his father had been a sheriff. But no, he had simply seen an article in the newspaper about the department accepting recruits and he needed a job.

They had begun to see each other while Joe was going through the police academy and it hadn't taken long before things had become serious. They'd married soon after he'd graduated.

Joe was a rookie cop and not making all that much in salary. Lillian had just begun a decorating business of her own. So they had decided to wait on starting a family until they were better situated financially. The wait stretched on and the idea of having children faded over time.

Although they considered themselves to be a happily married couple, should anyone have asked, their marriage had in fact become strained and spontaneous moments of happiness were seldom experienced. Lillian had brought up the subject with Joe but it was hard to get inside of him.

He had been a keeper of secrets as a child, some of which were a burden he carried to this day. And a load not only on him but prone to weigh on those around him.

She had often wondered if his reticence had to do with Viet Nam. Joe never talked about his time there but she suspected there were things he might not have wanted her to know and that she herself might not have wanted to hear, either.

Her father had been like that about the war. Close mouthed.

She and Joe eventually agreed that they needed some space. They weren't ready to divorce but would entertain a trial separation. No strings attached either. Just keep any dalliances to yourself. They were grownups, after all. That had been more than two years ago. And things couldn't have turned out better.

To their surprise, they'd quickly discovered that they were indeed a perfect couple as long as they lived apart. The thrill returned. They felt liberated. Going out for the most mundane reason was like a date. Romance showed up. The possibility of having a tryst with anyone else never went anywhere.

Friends and family were still trying to figure out their situation.

"How about we take in a movie tonight?" Lillian suggested.

"Sure. What do you want to see?"

"Well, Stripes is playing in town," she said. "Suppose to be funny."

"Might make me want to re-enlist," Joe laughed. "Got a few things to finish here. See you in about an hour."

~~~

Ricky Ricola's evening had begun with yet another bus ride, this time from his place to Chinatown where he'd hoped to make some fast money. Now he was standing on the sidewalk in front of a convenience store on Nu'uana Street rocking back and forth on his heels and having made no money of any kind yet. A passing car slowed and the passenger in the front seat cut his eyes at him. Ricky avoided looking back. He was starting to feel uncomfortable. He didn't have any experience in this kind of thing. He shouldn't be here. He should get back on the bus and go home.

Finding out what Frank had put in that locker at the bar had really rattled him. It was certainly something he wanted nothing more to do with, especially in light of the directions things have taken. He hadn't questioned Frank's explanation of why he wanted him to rent the lockers at the time. Nor the reason for that little chicanery he'd asked him to pull off with the keys at the bar. But his curiosity had gotten the best of him afterwards and before leaving he had gone in to take a look inside the other locker. And now Frank was dead. Dead under suspicious causes according to the police. That was even more frightening. Obviously, they were talking about murder. And worse, he had a good idea of who'd done it. And even more worse, he could identify him if pushed.

He had taken some of the drugs home and filled the little packets he'd gotten at the drugstore. He had no idea how much they would be worth on the street. Didn't matter, he'd be happy with anything. Just enough to get somewhere far, far away, that's all.

He wondered what time the next bus was?

"What's happening, man?"

Ricky turned to see a heavyset man with a shaved head and wearing an aloha shirt standing directly behind him. Another man, wiry and sporting a long ponytail, stood next to the man. He had on sunglasses, which he removed and placed in his pocket. His eyes were hard. Neither appeared to be tourists.

"Word is you're doing a little street business," the bald man grinned evilly, weighing a beefy hand on Ricky's shoulder. "That true?"

"I don't know what you're talking about," Ricky said, attempting to brush the had away.

"Maybe you don't understand the situation in this neighborhood," the man said, tightening his grip, the thumb painfully stabbing into Ricky's collarbone. "This part of town is taken. You're stepping on important toes just by showing your ugly face here."

The ponytailed man grabbed Ricky's other arm but he twisted away and turned to run. The only place open was the street.

One block down at the stoplight, Kedron Olomano sat behind the steering wheel in his souped-up Volkswagen Bug. The car's single exhaust pipe, pointing straight up like a scorpion's stinger, snarled as the engine revs increased. A tricked-out black Toyota pickup truck in the lane next to him began to race its engine. The light flashed to green and both vehicles bolted into the intersection. The VW got the jump.

Kedron was pulling ahead, his attention given to the engine tachometer which had redlined at the maximum revolutions, when out of the corner of his eye he saw a shadow dart out from the curb. He felt a bump and the steering wheel shuddered slightly. He momentarily took his foot off the gas pedal. The Toyota shot past him.

Kedron hung a right at the next corner and switched off the headlights. He could hear the front tire rubbing against something. Another quick turn took him to an empty street where he stopped. Outside of the car he discovered the expensive custom-made right front fender was badly dented. Whatever he'd flattened back there had obviously been bigger than a cat.

~~~

Joe wheeled his aging Honda Accord into the parking garage of the apartment building where Lillian lived in Kahala. It was in a top neighborhood.

When they had separated and had given up the rental they'd lived in then, she had decided to look in the neighborhood for an apartment. Her thinking had been that having a Kahala address might be good for business. She'd been able to haggle with the owner enough to knock the rent down to an acceptable amount.

Joe had gotten a break on his tiny studio as well. The management there had reasoned it might not be a bad idea to have a cop in residence.

Lillian could more than afford her place now. She often showed it to clients as an example of her work. The real thing was much better than looking at photographs. Lately, she'd been considering the idea of doing her business completely at home. Something exclusive about that, not to mention the tax break.

Joe had always loved the idea of her being there. Shacked up at a tony address, he liked to tease her about.

"Busy day tomorrow?" Lillian asked before getting out of the car.

"Not all that much," Joe shrugged. "Got a curious phone call I'm trying to run down."

"Sounds exciting." she said. "It's early yet, you know. The night is young and bad things await those who are lucky."

~~~

Detective Curtis Lam had drawn the night duty card at the Chinatown station when traffic requested the need for a detective at an accident scene. He took the call. After his preliminary investigation in which not a single witness had come forward, he'd driven to Queen's Medical hospital and was now sitting in the ER waiting room. A doctor entered and approached him.

"I'm Dr. Sheryl Kahale," she said. "I assume you're here about the hit-and-run?"

"Yes, I'm Detective Curtis Lam. I came here from the scene. How is he?"

"I head up emergency, detective," Dr. Kahale said. "The man didn't make it. In fact, he never regained consciousness. There was a severe head injury and I also suspect internal organ damage. That'll be determined by autopsy. However, I think you should see something. Please come with me."

She led him to a curtained off area where Ricky Ricola's nude and damaged body lay on a gurney. His clothes were in a laundry bag at his foot. She removed a small plastic bag from it stuffed full of glassine packets, each containing a white powder.

"We undressed him so we could better examine his injuries," she said. "This was stuck down the front of his underpants."

"Kind of unusual for a codpiece," Lam quipped. "But offhand, I'd say that powder looks like it might be heroin."

"I agree on both assessments," Dr. Kahale smiled. "We'll hold the body for the medical examiner. You can have the clothes for any kind of evidence they might provide. What do you want to do about the codpiece?"

"I can give it to our narcotics back at the station," Lam said. "Did he have any identification? I didn't check at the scene."

She reached in the bag again and handed him a billfold..

"Expired drivers license," Lam noted, flipping it open. "Says his name is Richard Ricola. Wonder if the address is still the same? Have to inform any family. As for the drugs, it'd be better if narcotics picked them up here. I'll give them a call and stick around until they arrive, if that's okay."

"That will be fine, detective," Dr. Kahale agreed. "Just keep out of the way if we get busy."

Lam nodded that he would and looked at the body.

"Could someone put a sheet over him?" he asked.

Chapter 5

"I left a message on Joe's machine," Albert said.

"Shouldn't you try him at the police station?" Helen asked.

"I don't have his number there. I'd have to check all over Honolulu."

"George will be buried in the ground before Joe even knows he's dead," Helen sighed.

"Joe will be here, don't worry. I'm going to Roberts and see how they're doing with George. They're expecting me. Should be back soon."

The funeral home was located across town, actually on a line directly opposite from the Cheo home. Several streets were still closed due to the storm flooding. Detours added an extra thirty minutes to the drive.

Bob Roberts, dressed in a dark blue suit and wearing a red tie with white polka dots, had been admiring his work in the sanctuary when Albert arrived. This was always a proud moment for him when the first visitor came, particularly when it was a member of the departed's family. It was something that only a colleague could fully understand.

"So, what do you think?" he asked. "Meet with your satisfaction?"

Roberts had chosen magenta filters for a soft lighting effect in the room. It complemented everyone's appearance, including the deceased.

George Cheo was laid out in a teak coffin of simple design and lined with a warm cream satin. Roberts preferred that color over the starker white. It was less clinical, he believed. A spray of flowers stood at each end.

George's hair had been stylishly set in a manner anyone else but him might have worn well. Makeup had been sparingly applied by Roberts himself to avoid giving even the slightest hint of a mannequin look. He'd been dressed in a vintage aloha shirt that Albert had chosen from George's wardrobe and chino pants with a sharp crease down each leg that Helen had ironed. He wore a new pair of brown leather shoes polished to a high sheen.

"I was thinking of having the funeral at home," Albert said, "but now perhaps having it at graveside would be better."

"We can arrange that," Roberts said. "It's a beautiful location. Or you might want to consider using our chapel. It has become popular lately."

"No, I like the idea of everything being outdoors. At least that's keeping a little with tradition. You know, once people buried only the bones of a family member. That was a sacred custom. It was called a clean burial. They believed it put the being or essence of the person back into the ground. That was a long time ago. Only native Hawaiians were here then."

Albert fancied himself as being quite knowledgeable in matters of tradition.

Roberts gave him a simpering little smile.

"I'd like to have a Mele Oli," Albert told him. "See to it."

"I know a very good person who can do the chant," Roberts said. "I'll call him right away and give him some information about George."

Albert placed a hand on his brother's shoulder before turning to leave.

"Do something about his hair," he said.

~~~

"Good morning, Detective Cheo," Lola Kahamena greeted, checking her watch and raising her eyebrows. "Guess it still is morning. Alarm clock didn't ring?"

Joe had just walked in. He held up his palms in surrender.

"What was the name of the fellow who called you?" she asked. "The fidgety one, remember?"

"Ricky Ricola," Joe said. "He call again?"

"I thought that name sounded familiar," Lola said. "No, he won't be calling. You'd better read the morning paper."

Joe signed in and went straight to his desk. As usual, Walt had left the paper there. The story was on the second page. A couple of moments later he was on the phone speaking with Detective Curtis Lam.

"A reporter was outside the emergency room nosing around," Lam said. "Guess he picked up on what'd happened. Got the vic's name from somebody there 'cause we wouldn't have released it without first informing the family. So you think this could be the same guy you're looking for?"

"Only Ricola I know," Joe said. "As far as his family goes, I'm not aware of any. At least he never mentioned them."

"His drivers license listed him as Richard Ricola," Lam said. "The license was expired."

"Not surprised about that. What address does it show?"

Lam read it off.

"That's his," Joe said. "Ricky was his nickname."

"I'll fax you a copy of the license," Lam said. "He really got creamed. ER doc told me he never regained consciousness. Felony hit-and-run now. Will go at least to manslaughter for sure. We've been through his apartment. Didn't find anything suspicious. You said he sounded nervous when he called you?"

"I never spoke with him," Joe said. "Department secretary took the call. Did anyone get a license plate?"

"You guys have a secretary, huh? Must be nice to have friends in high places. Negative on the plate. Guy in a convenience store said two cars might've been drag racing when it happened. He couldn't describe them other than they were loud, much less catch a plate. Said there's a lot of street racing in that area. Most witnesses vanished as soon as traffic patrol arrived. Not exactly a cop-friendly section of town. Lot of drug activity on the streets. Ricola might've been dealing. He had a bag of glassines on him filled with what our narcotics believes to be heroin. Narcotics is checking out where the batch might've come from. You know, who processed it. The raw stuff comes from Afghanistan where they grow the poppy plants. The bad guys get it for a song and then have it refined at a lab. Price goes way up when they sell it to the dealers. That's what I meant when I said nothing suspicious was in his apartment. Not that he would have had a lab there. But maybe a number on a scrap of paper. Even an address book."

"Dealing doesn't sound like Ricky," Joe said. "He wasn't a user much less a dealer. He was small time. Shoplifting, that sort of thing. I don't know, maybe he's changed. Everything else has. Still, I don't figure him for dealing drugs. He couldn't afford the price of admission to get into that game."

"Gets even better or worse depending on how you look at it. The bag of drugs was stuffed down the front of his shorts. Ten or twelve grams. I joked to the ER doctor about it being a codpiece."

"Guys always put a pair of socks down there to impress the girls when I was in junior high school," Joe laughed. "But here's an interesting thing. Probably just a coincidence but Ricola lived at the same apartment building as the victim in another death that's being considered suspicious. Don't know if drugs were involved there. Like I said, may be coincidental but it makes me wonder if there could be a connection between the two. That other death happened at the docks. Now Ricola turns up holding serious drugs. I'm going to mention this to the detectives handling the dock investigation. Since I knew Ricky, I'd like for us to keep in touch providing you're good with that."

"I don't have a problem. Might be helpful. I'm here because I was night dick and first on the scene and that makes me lead. Narcotics is covering the codpiece angle. Yeah, call me whenever you want. Be happy to talk or share, whatever."

Joe hung up and considered again the idea of a connection between Lofume and Ricola. They lived at the same address. Frank Lofume discovered dead in a parking lot near the docks. He'd have to find out the specifics on how he died. Illegal drugs often come in there by ship from overseas. Ricky Ricola dead with a bag of dangerous dope in his shorts. It's not that big of a stretch to think that something was going on between them. Few more pieces to put together on that, however. He dialed another number and hoped Tony Boyd was near the payphone.

"Yeah," a voice he recognized answered.

"Mr. Boyd, this is Detective Cheo. We spoke earlier."

"I remember. So why are you calling this time?"

"Unfortunately to tell you that Ricky Ricola was killed in an accident last night. Do you know if he has any family? They would need to be notified."

"So that's what happened to him, huh?" Boyd said. "Cops have been here half the morning going through his apartment. Same thing as they did with Lofume. Didn't say anything about him being dead, though. Just kept asking me about drugs. Told them I don't allow the damn stuff around here. They sure didn't find any, either. Probably pissed them off. Christ, that's two tenants gone. Place will be empty soon. No, Ricky never mentioned any family to me. Not that he had any reason to. Like I told you before, I stay out of other people's business."

"Wonder if I could come there and take a peek in his apartment?" Joe asked. "Maybe I could find a name of someone to call."

Joe realized he was stepping over a line. There were two investigations underway by different squads involving that building. Anything he might come across could be crucial evidence. Worse, it could be corrupted by him. Again, he'd better remember his place. Still, he was bored out of his skull.

"I guess that'd be okay," Boyd said.

"Thank you. I'll leave right now."

The drive to the apartment building didn't take long. Joe found a parking space a block past and walked back. A small sign inside the entrance listed the superintendent's apartment. It was down the hall next to the pay phone.

Boyd answered the door after the first knock.

"That was quick," he muttered.

"I'm Detective Joe Cheo. Sorry to meet under these conditions."

"Yeah, well, it wasn't like I knew the guy or we were pals. The apartment is on the second floor. Take the stairs. It's right at the head."

He handed Joe the key.

"Bring it back when you're done. That's the only extra I've got. Have to get a couple made before we rent it out again."

Joe was surprised that he had just handed over the key and was sending him on his way. He'd have thought that he would have insisted on coming with him. Still, he wasn't going to argue.

As soon as he opened the apartment door, he could see that the narcotic detectives had been busy. Things were knocked about. Drawers left open. Clothes strewn on the floor. But once inside and even with all the disorder, there was an odd air of tidiness. The carpet seemed recently vacuumed. No dusty corners. No greasy fingerprints staining the doorjambs. Ricky was apparently a good housekeeper. He doubted if he'd had a cleaning lady.

The furniture looked old and worn but yet serviceable. There was a living room with a sofa and a coffee table. An easy chair sat in a corner. A framed print of Diamond Head hung on one wall. The bedroom had a single bed, a chest of drawers and an armoire. No closet. A small kitchen with a four burner electric stove and a refrigerator. And a bathroom with a shower but not a tub. Not exactly a palace but a comfortable enough place to live. Even cozy.

Where to look first? A big help would've been if he had known what he was looking for. More to the point, anything that might've been useful would have obviously already been found. Which would be a lucky thing for him, considering.

For some reason he felt a little sad about all of the disarray. That gave him an idea. He would to do things in reverse order. Look while he straightened up. He slipped on a pair of gloves.

He put the cushions back on the sofa and chair after running his hand around the sides and back. As a final touch, he removed a wrinkle in the rug with his foot.

Next, he moved to the bedroom and started picking up things and placing them back where they belonged. Socks, underpants, tee-shirts and some odds and ends were neatly returned to the chest of drawers. He put a couple of slacks and a jacket on their hangers to go in the armoire, which strangely had a nice pair of dress shoes inside it. The bed was torn apart. He looked between the mattresses and on the floor beneath it. Nothing there. Then he made the bed.

The two kitchen cabinets were limited to a small collection of plates, three cups and a few canned goods. The apartment was starting to get back together.

Last stop was the bathroom.

The toilet was singing. He jiggled the handle to make it stop but that didn't help. He removed the top of the water closet and looked inside. Something on the bottom was keeping the flapper valve slightly open. He reached down and pulled it out. It was a key and it had a number and a large asterisk stamped on it.

He carefully put the key in an evidence envelope, slipped it in his pocket and left the apartment.

Instead of heading back to the station he drove home. Entering his own apartment he was reminded that his own housekeeping skills trended toward the lower side of tidiness. The bed was passably made, though. He saw that the answering machine on the table had a message. He pushed the play button.

Albert's voice came from the speaker. It sounded tinny.

'Joe, this is your Uncle Albert. Your father has died. The funeral is the day after tomorrow. You need to be here.'

Stated as matter-of-factly as that. He sat down on the bed.

Strangely, he felt a certain amount of relief. He'd broken with his family years ago after returning from the war, although he had since discovered that you're never completely free of the past. Perhaps this was a beginning?

He'd call Albert for more details. And Lillian. She should come with him. But he wouldn't blame her if she refused. Maybe she could make airline reservations for them. Should they stay at a hotel or the house? He'd think about that later. First, he had to request a few days leave.

Chapter 6

Lillian had instantly agreed to come with Joe and had mildly reprimanded him for even thinking that she might not have. No decision had been made as to where they might stay during the visit, however. Better to wait until they get there.

Now the flight attendant was rushing to complete the refreshment service during the short hop from Honolulu to Kona.

"Something to drink, ma'am?" she asked.

"No, thanks," Lillian said.

"Would the gentleman care for anything?" the attendant quietly asked her.

Joe had dozed off.

"Let him sleep," Lillian whispered. "He's probably in the middle of a pleasant dream."

* * *

The field of fire wasn't very good, two hundred plus yards across an area of low elephant grass, as seen through a break in the foliage from their position in the tree line. The grass had begun to sway in a small shifting breeze, so windage might also be a problem. But they would have to make do. The two-man recon team didn't dare go any nearer for fear of being spotted.

Joe brought up his binoculars and swept the village. There was little movement but he thought he could hear voices. Then he spotted two figures standing in the shadows in front of a straw hooch. He brought them closer and sharpened the focus.

"Just to the left of that last hooch," he whispered to his parter. "Two people. Ours is the caucasian guy."

"Got him," his partner whispered back, viewing the man in the telescopic sight mounted on the rifle, its crosshairs centered directly on the target's forehead. "Take the shot?"

"Do it," Joe said tightly, his whole body tense.

The man Joe held in his binoculars now seemed to be looking back at him when he disappeared in a spray of red mist.

The boom of the gun released a clamor of hoots and yips in the surrounding foliage. Birds chattering noisily flew from the tree above them and circled. Joe and his teammate crouched and quickly backed farther into the cover. They turned and began to run. Small branches whipped at Joe's face as the two soldiers pushed through the brush. Joe stopped momentarily and could hear nothing. No one was following. Now feeling safer they hurried on to the pickup location.

Soon the heavy twup-twup of rotor blades resounded. The helicopter came into view and hovered above the small clearing. Normally it would have dropped a penetrator but instead of the metal cage designed to cut through jungle canopy and in which they could've strapped themselves, only a rope fell from the hovering chopper's door. Joe wasn't going to argue, though. He grabbed the line, looped it around his partner and signed for them to wench him up.

The soldier safely aboard, the rope dropped again for Joe.

He was just a few feet from the welcoming door when the round smacked into his thigh. Then several more bullets peppered the bottom of the chopper. The ground fire intensified and he was hit again. Another bullet creased the left cheek of his face.

The chopper nosed over and began a steep emergency climb with Joe in tow fluttering like a balloon on a string. He slipped into unconsciousness to the deafening sound of the turbine engines and the smell of burning jet fuel.

* * *

The tires squeaked to awaken Joe as the airliner touched down smoothly at Keahole Airport. As the engines reversed thrust noisily, Joe could smell the burning of jet fuel. They'd arrived in Kona.

~~~

""Have you found out anything?" Albert asked.

"Nothing yet," Tiny said. "No word on the street, either. Kind of funny. If somebody was selling it around here, you'd know."

Albert had earlier called Tiny to come to the house. He had taken him out to the ohana where they could talk more freely.

"This can't wait much longer," Albert grumbled.

"I'm nosing around," Tiny said.

Albert glared at him.

"You aren't listening to what I'm saying, Tiny. I can't afford to let this go on forever. I don't want nosing around. I want a goddamn name! I want results! Do you understand?"

"I'll talk with the crew again," Tiny stuttered nervously. "Somebody might slip up. Or I could've missed something the last time. It's just…"

Tiny's breath began to heave. Albert realized that was all he was going to get for now. He'd come back to it later.

"Okay, look into that," he said calmly. "Now, on to another subject. Joe's arriving today. Plane should've already landed. While he's here I'm going to offer him a job."

"Joe?" Tiny said in surprise. "But isn't he a cop?"

"Everybody's something once, Tiny. That's how you get experience. George's passing has caused me to think of the future. It's time to bring this family together. We've been divided for too long."

"But I thought there was bad feelings between you and Joe," Tiny said.

"Blood runs thick in our family," Albert smiled.

~~~

Joe had treated himself by renting a red Buick Riviera convertible at the airport. Now with the top down, he and Lillian were cutting across the island on Saddle Road, a narrow two-lane highway over the mountain that ties Kona to Hilo. The highway had been built years ago and was in sore need of repair. Joe had to sweet talk the car rental agent into letting him come this way. Normally, the companies won't allow their cars up here. He'd been in luck since the agency was an independent. The national rentals wouldn't have allowed him.

It is a beautiful and frightening landscape, a place of beginnings and endings. An occasional living tree grown from a seed brought in on the wind holds stubbornly to the black lava while the bone-white limb of another tree now dead reaches from the sinewy twists and folds.

Old tales and superstitions abound. People have told of seeing lights floating over the knife-sharp rock. Madame Pele herself has reportedly been seen wandering among the outcrops.

"How lovely," Lillian said dreamily. "All that lava flowing everywhere. I can't image how it must've looked then."

"You wouldn't have wanted to have been here," Joe said. "That stuff can move faster than you'd think. It's called au'au' lava after it cools. Know why?"

"Okay, why?"

"It has sharp edges and that's what you say when you step on it barefooted," Joe laughed.

"That's a terrible joke," Lillian said, laughing herself.

"Lucky we got good weather," Joe said. "It can shut down in a minute up here. Can't see a thing. We're over a mile high at this point. Sometimes you're even in the clouds."

"Then we'd just have to pull over and snuggle."

"Don't give me any ideas," Joe said.

Lillian glanced at him, his black hair blowing. She liked that he was wearing it longer. It suited his face. She hoped some dumb department regulation wouldn't make him cut it.

"This baby probably has weather radar as standard equipment," Joe said. "That'd get us through the soup."

"You look good in this car," Lillian told him. "You should sell that old beater you drive and buy one of these."

"Are you kidding?" Joe laughed. "You know what this thing costs? Besides, half the department already thinks I'm on the take because of who I am. They see me tooling around in a hot new convertible and they'd go bananas."

"Well, you and I know you aren't on any kind of take."

"Internal affairs would probably be waiting for me as soon as I pulled into the parking lot."

"It's not only stupid but unfair," Lillian said angrily.

"Fairness has nothing to do with it. It's their job to be suspicious. Especially when your name happens to be Cheo."

"That's what I mean about being unfair, Joe. We've talked about this a hundred times."

"Well, maybe things will lighten up now that there's one less Cheo."

"It's sad, really, that you even have to think like that," Lillian said. "I wish it were different for you."

"Me, too," Joe said. "When I worked patrol it wasn't so bad. Yeah, some guys would joke about my family background. I'd tell them that's why I became a cop. And they could fuck off if they had a problem. Never any really hard feelings from the troops, though detectives has gotten uptight lately. I think it's coming from the brass. Beyond me why or what it's about but they busted me to auto thefts. Maybe just a wild hair but there you are. Sometimes I think I would've been better off staying with patrol."

"Can you go back there?" Lillian asked. "To patrol?"

"Be unusual," Joe said. "Don't know if anyone's ever done that. Probably need a lot of pull. That lets me out."

"Might be worthwhile to look into it," Lillian said. "I mean, if you think that would make you happy."

"I'd rather stick around detectives and beat them at their own game," Joe grinned.

Lillian turned and looked out the passenger window.

"How long before we're there?" she asked.

"About another half hour. Maybe a little longer."

Chapter 7

"Come in, come in," Albert boomed happily.

Joe and Lillian entered the house.

"Hello, dears," Helen called softly from the sofa.

"Hi, mom," Joe said, walking over and bussing her on the cheek.

"Oh, Joe," she said tearfully, taking his hand in hers, "It has been so long."

Joe felt a rush of guilt. He cursed himself for having it.

"Can't be helped, mom."

"I like your car," Albert said, noticing the Buick before shutting the door. "Pretty fancy for a rental."

"It's all they had," Joe said.

"You should've come in to General Lyman airport here. I could have picked you up. Wouldn't have needed a car."

"The connection from Honolulu was better going to Kona."

"Which way did you come, Joe? Around the coast?"

"We took Saddle Road from the airport."

"Dangerous road," Albert said gravely. "Bad weather can fall on you in a minute. Lots of accidents up there."

"The weather was perfect. No traffic at all."

"I'll put on some coffee," Helen said, getting up from the sofa.

"Let me help you," Lillian said, seizing the opportunity. "It'll give us a chance to talk."

The two women left the room. The men stood in silence.

"Place looks about the same," Joe finally spoke.

"Lot of memories here," Albert said. "Brings back some good times. Really glad you came, Joe. Even if had to be under this sad situation. Are you and Lillian's things in the car? We can go get them."

"We haven't made up our minds where we're staying yet," he said. "We might try a hotel."

"Don't be silly, Joe," Albert admonished. "We have plenty of room. You mother would be hurt if you went elsewhere."

Joe wondered about that. He now realized there had always been a little coolness between Lillian and Helen. He suspected it was because Lillian was a haole girl. His mother wasn't above showing some bias against non-native Hawaiians. Also, she had never understood nor accepted the idea that he and Lillian could live apart and remain married. She was certain that something distasteful had to be behind it.

"I guess you're right," Joe resignedly agreed rather than argue. "But don't bother with the bags. There're just two overnights. I'll get them later."

Helen and Lillian came in with the fresh coffee. Joe noticed his mother had a slight grimace. Lillian shot him an exasperated look.

"Nothing like a hot cup of Kona coffee," Albert said, taking in the aroma.

It reminded Joe of the Sunrise Cafe in Honolulu and how he wished he were there right now.

"After everyone has rested, we'll drive over to Roberts," Albert said.

~~~

Joe held his mother's arm as they entered the sanctuary. Albert supported her by the other arm. Lillian followed behind them.

The disbelief of hearing that someone has died ends the moment you see the body. It removes any and all doubt.

The coffin was entirely open. Its top removed.

Joe felt his breath shorten. He was taken with how small his father looked and how closely he fitted inside the coffin. He wondered if they should have gotten a larger one. Something roomier. He placed his hand on his father's forehead. The skin felt cold and waxy beneath his touch. A profound sadness welled up within him.

"That was his favorite shirt," Albert commented.

"I'm glad he's wearing it," Joe said.

Then he took another look at the shirt.

"Where did that come from?" he asked.

Joe pointed to the medal pinned on the left front pocket.

"The Army gave it to him after the war," Albert said.

"That's the Bronze Star," Joe said. "It's awarded for meritorious service in combat."

Albert shrugged.

"He never said what they gave it to him for," he said. "I just thought it would look good on him."

Another wave of sadness passed over Joe. How little he knew about his dad. Maybe the Army has a record of the medal's citation, he thought. He could research that. Maybe.

Helen stood quietly, her eyes fixed on the face she so often had held. Lillian slipped her arm around her waist to offer comfort.

"I need to see Roberts about tomorrow," Albert announced. "I'd appreciate it if you would come with me, Joe. We won't be long."

Joe nodded.

"Mainly, I wanted to talk with you," Albert whispered confidentially, after they'd left the sanctuary. "Let's go out front."

Joe squinted as his eyes adjusted to the bright sunlight.

"How's the police business?" Albert asked.

"Thriving."

"They treating you all right? I mean, things are going okay?"

"Just get to the point, Albert."

"The family is the point, Joe. There are only the two of us now. It's time we settled our differences. Get this family back together."

"I don't see how that's possible," Joe scoffed. "We live in different worlds, Albert. And frankly, I have no interest in being in any part of yours."

"I suspected you might feel that way," Albert said. "Actually, I'm not surprised. Yes, our worlds may seem to be different at times but they're not really when you look at the total picture and carefully examine it. The problem starts when we think there are only two sides to everything. Good and bad. Occasionally those sides can switch places and one becomes the other. And you don't even realize what has happened. Life is funny. You can't be sure of anything. Let me tell you a story."

"I'd really like to get back inside, Albert."

"Remember the Hawaiian word for uncle?" Albert asked. "It's anakala. So indulge your old Anakala Albert for just a little longer."

"All right but keep it short."

"Thank you," Albert said with a slight bow of his head. "When your mother and George were married, they planned to have children. Kids and more kids. Everyone had a big family then. It was expected. But none came. Both Helen and George were disappointed. George wondered if she were infertile. Perhaps she'd been injured some way in the tsunami. She wondered herself after he'd brought it up. They both agreed that it was a bad thing but it had to be accepted. One day a man, Kimo Kaohelaulii was his name, approached George with a question. He asked him how Hawaiian he was. George didn't know how to answer that. Now the Kaoheluliis were poor people but they were blessed with a wealth of children. So Kimo told him that he was thinking about hanai. That's the Hawaiian way of spreading the blessings of family."

"I'm familiar with hanai," Joe said, thinking of course his mother would've been blamed for infertility. God forbid anything be wrong with his father.

"Yes, those fortunate enough to have children often give a child to another family less fortunate as an act of love."

"Or one less mouth to feed," Joe said.

"George went home to talk the idea over with Helen," Albert said, ignoring the sarcasm. "And she told him that she was pregnant. She'd been keeping it as a surprise. See how things balance out? Something that was considered bad before had now become good. And it was a special blessing because you had been such a big baby she could never have another."

That guilt trip had been laid on Joe ever since he could remember. It still hurt.

"Now the scales are open again," Albert said. "Something bad has happened and the family has taken a sad loss. It is a tough blow but it offers an opportunity to make something good of that and rebalance the scale. Joe, I'd like you to come work with me. Together we can build the family back. Even stronger this time."

"Together? Something good? This family has always been dirty. Everyone knows that. My friends, when I was in school, used to tease me about it. Called us the Cheo mob. And incidentally, don't forget you who you're talking to now. I'm a cop, remember?"

"And don't you forget who you are, Joe," Albert shot back. "You belong to this family, like it or not. It's in your blood. You are a Cheo."

"I'm going inside."

"Ask yourself where you'll be ten years from now," Albert persisted. "Probably retired on a little pension and making ends meet doing security at a shopping mall. You deserve better. And you can have it better starting right now. Don't let past judgements cloud your thinking."

"My thinking is absolutely clear, Albert."

"I'm glad to hear that because there's another reason why you should consider what I'm offering. This belongs on that good side you're so concerned about. I've heard there's a real chance for gambling to be approved this year. That's on good authority, mind you. It'll mean more jobs for everyone. I've looked into it and made inquiries. I've also learned that some hotels are for sale around the islands. A group of businessmen is forming to buy them. Some powerful people are involved and I may be invited to join them. The details are being worked out. It is an entirely new venture. The hotels will have casinos. That's where I'd like to involve you, Joe. To run the entire security operation. This is going to be big and you can get in at the beginning. Keep your job for now. That would even be better while we're getting everything up and running. What do you say?"

"There you two are," Lillian said, opening the door and stepping outside. "I was looking all over. Helen would like to go home now."

"We're finished here," Joe said.

"Get your mother," Albert told him. "I do need to speak to Roberts. Have to make sure the chanter is here early tomorrow. Keep in mind our conversation, Joe. Some important things are about to change. You might want to hear more about them before making a decision."

Everyone retired early that night. Albert went to the ohana. Joe and Lillian sacked out on the living room sofa. Hellen slept alone in her empty bed.

Chapter 8

Chants are akin to the lyrics of a song. They rise and fall in harmonic emphasis to tell stories of courage and love. They give thanks. They can be personal. Even intimate. But however lovely they sound, they must always be truthful.

The Chanter knows this and chooses the aloha words of his prayer only after great consideration because once used they can never be taken back. They belong to the wind.

The gentlest curl of a breeze catches the uppermost branch of the huge banyan tree standing in the cemetery where George Cheo's life is set to song. It stirs the leaves before joining the stream of air flowing above Hilo on its journey to the other islands and beyond.

Voices in the wind.

~~~

"You sure you're okay about leaving?" Lillian asked. "We can stay until tomorrow."

Joe had given their goodbyes after the funeral. He and Lillian were now on their way to the airport.

"They won't miss us," he said. "The house will be full of visitors for the rest of the day. Probably half the night, too. Lot of stories yet to be told."

"I suppose you're right," Lillian agreed. "At least I won't have to be around that huge man they call Tiny any longer. He scares me. Does he have a real name?"

Joe laughed.

"Yeah, but just to get a drivers license. All he's ever gone by is Tiny. He's just a washed-up old thug. Don't worry about him. He's harmless. Gets a little addled sometimes, is all."

"If you say so," Lillian said. "Everyone else at the funeral seemed so nice. Some even joked and laughed. I thought that was kind of unusual considering, well, where we were and why we were there and all."

"Hawaiian funerals are different that way," Joe explained. "Sure, there might be a few wet eyes and some hankies pulled out but there's nothing disrespectful about having a good laugh among friends."

"So this old washed-up thug, is he a family friend?"

"Albert's friend. They have being has-beens in common."

"What's the story behind that?"

"Albert was mixed up briefly with a really bad criminal gang in the Sixties," Joe said. "Those guys were into extortion, drugs, illegal gambling, even murder. Not just here on Hawaii but throughout the other islands, as well. Probably had someone like Albert working for them there, too. Just another local lackey. Not sure what he expected to gain in the association. He was way out of his league with this bunch. Would've been more to my grandfather's liking if he'd been around. Anyway, Tiny was supposedly one of the gang's muscles. His size alone was intimidating enough. He hardly ever needed to get into any rough stuff. When most of the gang finally killed each other off or were sent to prison, the whole thing sort of fell apart and dissolved. Tiny wasn't of any interest to the police. Albert took him in and simply continued doing what he'd always done. Union payoffs, construction graft, little smuggling, setting up illegal card games. Small potatoes in the overall crime scale."

"Fascinating," Lillian said. "And that's what is forever holding you back. Small potatoes. Even though you were never involved in anything with anyone. Again, I know we've talked about this but apparently it still bothers you. And, yes, I admire your principles and understand your sensitivity but do you think perhaps you've gone a little overboard about this whole Cheo thing?"

"I don't know. Maybe you're right. Could be what's holding me back is I'm not as good of a cop as I think. Maybe the writing has been on the wall all along and I never bothered to read it."

"Stop being silly. You know better. As for the other thing, people like to gossip. Even cops. Frankly, I think that the idea of anyone being serious about this because of your family name is all in your head."

"Could be that, too" he said. "Anyway, if they fire me, I can go to work for Albert. He actually offered me a job yesterday. Wants us to kiss and make nice."

"My God, what did you tell him?"

"Just repeated what I'd said before. I'd already told him he could stuff any idea of me coming back to Hilo and working for him."

"I don't know whether to laugh, cry or scream." Lillian said.

"How about we both just scream?" Joe yelled. "Who's going to hear us out here? Besides, it might feel good."

"You're on," Lillian yelled back.

And with the top down and both of them screaming at the top of their lungs, the car crested Saddle Road and continued on its way back to Kona.

Chapter 9

"Detective Cheo, got a minute?" Lieutenant Ito called from his office.

Joe had just walked into the detectives' room. He and Lillian had caught the last flight from Kona the night before. He'd stayed at her place in Kahala and had come to work straight from there.

"Have a seat," Ito gestured. "How was the funeral?"

"It was a ball," Joe said, sitting down.

"Pardon?"

""Everything went fine," Joe said. "Thank you."

"Good. I see auto theft's a little quiet. Take a look at these. Homicide passed them on."

Joe brightened. Could this finally be a break, he wondered?

"Sure," he said enthusiastically.

Ito shoved a stack of papers on his desk over to him.

"They are all preliminary investigation reports patrol took," he said. "Mostly simple assaults. Battery detective has been out on sick leave and patrol gave them to homicide. I'd like you to write up the forms for each one and then run whatever seems worthy over to the city attorney for court filing."

Joe felt his face fall. Some break, he thought. A bunch of boring misdemeanors nobody wants to deal with. But why him?

"Something the matter?" Ito asked.

"No, I was just wondering why homicide couldn't have just handled it at the time. Doesn't look like that many."

"They've been busy," Ito said. "Your case load is light. This is a better allocation of manpower. Okay?"

"Yes, sir," Joe said. "I'll get right on it."

Walt Douglas was at his desk when Joe returned.

"Sorry about your dad," he said.

"Thank you. It's good to be back."

"What have you got there?"

"Somebody else's shit Ito dumped on me," Joe said sourly.

"He only does that because you're so tall and he's on the stumpy side. Maybe you should stoop over when you talk with him. Make him feel more comfortable. Make you appear more humble, too."

"Go screw yourself," Joe laughed. "Actually, I think it's more about Viet Nam. I understand he was an anti-war protester. We were all baby killers, you know. Anything new happen while I was away?"

"One thing," Walt said. "That DB they found in that parking lot in Pearl out near the docks? The suspicious death? It's a homicide now. Story's in this morning's paper."

"Really?" Joe said. "I haven't had a chance to read the paper. How was he killed? Shot? Stabbed?"

"He had a broken neck. They've kept that information to themselves for the time being. Just reported that it was now ruled a homicide. I got the info about the neck from a friend."

"That's a novel way to kill somebody," Joe said. "Maybe it was an accident. Possible, no?"

"Not a tree in sight he could've fallen from if that's what you mean," Walt said.

"What was he doing in the parking lot?" Joe asked.

"Probably getting his car. They found it parked there."

"Was it robbery?"

"Had his billfold on him. Full of cash. The car was locked."

"Maybe he was with a friend and they were horsing around," Joe offered. "You know, wrestling or something. Guy got scared and ran. Or he just stumbled. People have bad falls all the time. "

"Medical examiner believes otherwise," Walt said. "Judging from how the victim's neck was snapped, he says it's pretty conclusive that a gorilla got ahold of him. They can tell things like that."

"Narrows down the suspect list," Joe said.

"Yeah, they're checking with the zoo," Walt said. "Expect to make an announcement any minute now."

Both shared a laugh.

"Thing that's interesting to me is the dead guy and my old snitch, who's now also dead, lived at the same address," Joe said.

"You think there's some connection?" Walt asked.

"I just think it's curious," Joe told him. "Don't know what homicide thinks.

He wondered if he should mention that he'd been to Ricola's apartment? He decided not to for now.

"So what's the deal with those papers you've got?" Walt asked.

"PIRs that patrol wrote and gave to homicide because the person that should've gotten them bailed out sick and now I'm blessed with the job of getting them ready to take over for filing."

"Well, don't let me keep you from that," Walt said. "I know you just can't wait to get started. Anyway, I've got some running-around work to do and then I'm meeting Bee for lunch, so maybe I'll see you later. Have fun."

Joe straightened the stack of papers, then chewed on his pencil in frustration.

Finally accepting the fact that there was nothing he could do to get out of the lousy job, he read through the first report—a verbal disagreement between a couple, the woman was allegedly pushed. No mention of injury but it could be considered battery. He wrote it up and started on the next one, a juvenile issue. Daughter sassed her mom.

His mind drifted to the Lofume homicide. He went back over what he knew.

The victim lived in the same building as did Ricky Ricola, so they had to have known each other even it were just in passing. That given, what if there was more going on between them than just a casual hello? What did they have in common? Ricky was an opportunist. He was always looking to make a few quick bucks. He'd had serious drugs on him when he died and was presumed to have been dealing. Joe has to admit that that was a possibility, no matter how distant.

Frank Lofume must've worked at the docks. He could've been off a ship. The idea of him bringing in illegal drugs wasn't all that farfetched. He wondered if he could find out the ship's name? Would knowing that even matter? Probably not.

And then there's the cause of Lofume's death. Somebody wrung his neck as easily as it if had been a chicken's. Not an everyday event. Doesn't leave much in the way of evidence, either. He remembered hearing something about an old Hawaiian martial art called Kapu Ku'ilalua that specialized in bone breaking. Should they be looking for an old Hawaiian?

What was the motive? An argument that went too far? Or something else?

Homicide in that district has probably already looked into this. What he had to say was just speculation anyway. He doubted if they would even have been interested in hearing his idea of the two deaths possibly being connected. Probably don't even know about Ricky's death. The hell with it.

But his gut was telling him that there was a connection between them somewhere and somehow. And there is that damn key he found hidden in Ricky's toilet. Where did it fit in?

He picked up another report, this time a battery. The suspect allegedly shoved the victim for cutting in line at a movie theater.

~~~

"I suppose Joe and Lillian got home all right," Helen said. "I wish they could've stayed a little longer."

"Joe needed to get back to work," Albert said.

They were in the living room of the main house.

"So many visitors last night," Helen sighed. "I thought they'd never leave."

"George was an important man on the island," Albert said. "It was natural that people would want to come and pay their respect."

"I think it was because they didn't want to miss a party," Helen laughed.

"Well, I have to admit there's some truth in that," Albert chuckled.

"Well, George would have certainly enjoyed it," Helen said. "What should I do with all of his things, Albert? There are closets full of clothes and stuff."

"I don't know," Albert said. "The Salvation Army might take them. First, though, you should go through everything and see what you'd want to keep."

"Yes, there's some jewelry. And a few other things now that I think about it. I wonder if Joe would like to have something? A keepsake of his father."

"You could call him. Wait, there's an old surfboard George had. One of the first boards they made out of foam, if I remember correctly. Joe might like to have that. I think it's still around here somewhere. If I can find it, I'll send it to him."

"That would be wonderful, Albert. And yes, I will give George's things to the Salvation Army. That's a good idea. I'll ask Lucy Amito to come over and help me gather them up. I'd better ask Mrs. Hamakua, as well. She's too old to do much except get in the way but she would be hurt if I didn't."

"I'll also get out of your way," Albert said. "I have to go meet Tiny."

~~~

Joe had finished laying out the elements of the crimes for possible filing and had called the city attorney's office only to find out that no one could see him today. He made an appointment for the next morning.

He looked around the room. Couple other detectives there. The lieutenant was out of his office. Walt was gone. This would be a good time for him to get away himself. He stuck the forms in his desk drawer and locked it.

"I'm going to lunch," he said as he passed Lola's desk.

She waved goodbye and continued with her phone conversation.

Someone had drawn a cartoon vaguely resembling the lieutenant on the chalkboard. Joe laughed to himself and left without signing out.

He drove over to Waikiki, where there was a lunch wagon just off Kallpahulu that served a good plate meal. That particular wagon was pretty popular. He hoped they wouldn't be too busy and he'd have a long wait.

Most of the lunch crowd had thinned out by the time Joe arrived but luckily there was still some slow-roasted kalua pork left and he was given a huge serving along with the usual two scoops of steamed rice and a mayonnaise-laden macaroni salad.

Unable to take on another calorie after finishing the plate, he went for a brisk walk around the block.

Back in his car he decided to visit Tony Boyd. He wouldn't bother to call ahead. Why risk being put off?

~~~

Albert and Tiny sat on a bench in a small park at the harbor. A homeless man slumbered nearby under a palm tree.

"Interesting story in the newspaper this morning," Albert said. "You see it?"

"I don't read the newspapers," Tiny said and looked away.

Albert wondered if the man even could read. Probably only at a lower level. He'd never thought about that before, not that it mattered.

"This was in the Star-Bulletin," he told him. "Honolulu's paper has more news in it than ours. I like to read it occasionally but haven't had a chance to read anything for the past few days because of being so busy with the funeral. I thought that turned out well, wouldn't you say?"

Tiny didn't say. He had begun to sweat. Not only because of the sun but because he was still puzzled over why Albert wanted to see him here instead of at the ohana.

"The story I'm talking about had to do with Frank Lofume," Albert continued breezily. "I must say I was surprised by it. Actually, a little shocked. That's why I suggested we come to the park and talk instead of back at the house. Helen's having friends over."

"Frank was in the newspaper?" Tiny asked.

"Yes, he's dead."

Tiny paled.

"You look like you've seen a ghost," Albert noted. "Excuse me for a minute."

He got up and went over to where the homeless man was sleeping and stuck a five dollar bill in his shirt pocket.

"One good turn," he commented, returning and sitting down again. "Remember that, Tiny."

""I swear Frank was okay when I left him," Tiny said and took in a deep breath, "What happened?"

"Frank was found dead near the docks the morning after you left. In a parking lot, according to the paper. The police thought it was a suspicious death then. Now they're saying he was murdered."

Tiny seemed perplexed. He began to hyperventilate.

"Somebody killed him?" he said, swiping at his brow. "I don't understand. Why would anybody want to do that?"

Albert studied Tiny for a moment.

"I wonder why myself," he said. "Let's go back over the very last time you and Frank were together. Just this once more in case there's some small thing you might've forgotten. Start from where you and Frank loaded the crate on to the tug.

"We stowed the crate. And then we got off. Oh, yeah, Frank forgot his seabag. He went back for it."

"How long before Frank returned?" Albert asked.

"I don't know. Not long. Five or ten minutes maybe?"

Albert let out a breath.

"Five or ten minutes," he repeated.

"No more than fifteen," Tiny confirmed. "I'm sure."

And there it was, Albert realized, the small thing that'd been forgotten.

"You waited on the dock until he returned?" he asked.

Tiny nodded that he had.

"When did you first ask Frank to help you?"

"After you told me the drugs were coming and I'd have to get them. I figured this was important and I wanted to make sure nothing bad would happen."

"So Frank knew a couple of days in advance," Albert said. "That right?"

"Yeah, he said it was a good idea to have some protection and he'd be glad to help."

Albert wondered who else was involved in helping?

"All right, what have you found out?" he asked.

"I talked to the crew again. Got nothing. That union replacement checked out okay. Looked at the manifest, too. They might not have written down a pickup, though."

"What's a pickup?" Albert asked.

"Sometimes a person can work as a deckhand for a ride to another island," Tiny explained. "Just for the one trip."

"Is this so-called pickup someone they would know?"

"Not all the time."

Albert couldn't believe this.

"Go back and talk with everyone again," he snapped. "Find out about that pick up. Get me a name. You understand what I'm saying? I want a goddamn name!"

"I think so," Tiny said.

"Make sure you do," Albert told him firmly. "No mistakes. Get it right. Now, let's forget about Frank for the moment. The more important thing is my drugs are still missing. They aren't on the street. Not here or anywhere else. I'd know about it if they were. So whoever's responsible for stealing them could give them back. No questions asked. I would simply consider it a good turn. Why, there could even be a nice reward. Mention that as you ask around."

Tiny nodded.

"Now, back to Frank," Albert said. "He was a friend of Hugo and Pepe before he came to work for us, right?"

"He was mainly Pepe's friend."

"I knew Hugo when he lived in Honolulu but I didn't know Pepe all that much," Albert said. "Pepe lives here now but Frank lived in Honolulu. But though on different islands, they all remained friends, didn't they?"

"Yes, they were tight."

"Why, that's exactly right, Tiny. "Tight friends. I'd like you to pay Pepe a visit for me."

Chapter 10

"Sorry to disturb you, Mr. Boyd," Joe said. "I was in the neighborhood and wondered if you could help me again."

"Are you guys ever going to stop bugging me?" Boyd asked. "Okay, what do you need?"

"I understand how you must feel and the department appreciates your cooperation, sir," Joe said. "The last time I was here you let me see Ricky Ricola's apartment. That was a really big help. This time it concerns Frank Lofume. I realize the other officers have already been through his apartment but I'd also like to see his place if you have a moment."

"Well, you better take a good look while you can," Boyd told him. "Owner doesn't like vacancies. Been bugging me to get them rented. I'm putting out a sign tomorrow. That is, unless you and your buddies have a problem with that. Let me get the key."

"Thank you, I don't have a problem. This shouldn't take long."

"Upstairs two doors down from Ricola's old place," Boyd said, returning with the key and handing it to him.

Joe smiled. Luck was still with him. He mounted the stairs and went to the apartment. He started to put the key in the lock when he noticed the door hadn't been completely pulled shut. He hesitated and listened carefully. Hearing no movement from inside, he slowly pushed it open and cautiously stepped in.

~~~

'The door doesn't appear to have been forced open," Walt Douglas said, examining the lock. "Nothing's broken that I can see. Maybe the cops just forgot to lock up when they left. You said the building manager told you they'd been here. Or could the maid have absentmindedly left it open? Naw, I doubt if this place offers much in the way of maid service. I suppose the lock could've been picked but that takes a special skill. Couldn't tell if it had been anyway. Offhand and for the lack of anything more substantial, I'd just call this a suspicious entrance and be done with it."

Joe had indeed checked with Boyd about anyone other than the police having been in the apartment or asking questions and had gotten a definite no for an answer to both. Yet there was no denying that someone other than officers had been inside obviously looking for something. Even the cops wouldn't have left it that messed up. That's when he decided to call Douglas and had asked him to come there.

He'd been toying with the idea of taking Walt into his confidence. He was in over his head. He needed to talk with someone he could trust. A fellow officer. A friend. Tell him everything he'd learned so far concerning the two deaths. He could only guess at how that might set with him. He would just have to take the chance.

This snooping around that he was doing was reckless to say the least. Could've even been illegal in some instances. Certainly would get the department's back up. He had no right to involve his friend and put his job in jeopardy. Walt already had enough risk to worry about in another personal matter. He didn't need this one to add to it. His own job security, however, was fast approaching the no-return point at the rate he was going. Was he willing to continue?

"You have to get back to the station right away? I wouldn't mind stopping for a cup of coffee somewhere."

"Good idea," Walt said. "Then maybe you can explain what this cockamamie business of yours is all about."

The apartment building wasn't too far from the Sunrise Cafe. Joe suggested they drive there. Walt followed in his car.

"Best coffee in town," Joe said, after they'd been seated. "The banana bread's a treat, too. They bake it themselves."

Joe ordered for both of them and then sat for a moment tapping out a little rhythm with his fingers. He cleared his throat.

"I might be getting myself into a little trouble with the department, Walt. I was wondering if you'd like to join me."

~ ~ ~

A rain shower had fallen earlier that evening, lowering the humidity and refreshing the air. Joe sat on his balcony enjoying the cool night.

He wasn't all that knowledgeable about wine. If it poured he drank it. But he had splurged on a nice chianti before coming home. He filled his glass.

His talk with Walt Douglas hadn't gone as badly as he'd feared, though not as well as he'd perhaps hoped.

Douglas had patiently listened to every word without interrupting, other than to give an occasional grunt followed by a sad shake of his head. In the end, he had chided him mainly for not going through channels if he'd believed he had something pertinent to an investigation. But he had also said that he couldn't blame him, especially in light of the treatment he'd been given by the department—particularly Lieutenant Ito—and the fact that he'd known one of the victims. Just be careful he'd cautioned. The lieutenant wouldn't be so understanding.

Well, that was good enough for him and he had thanked his friend. He took a sip of wine. Wasn't bad.

The only thing he hadn't mentioned in their discussion was the key he'd taken from Ricky Ricola's apartment. He'd save that for later. If it became necessary, that is.

Overall, he felt better. Everything had become too big to keep inside any longer. To what extent his fellow officer would actually become involved in this clandestine investigation was still open to question.

The phone rang. He'd brought it out on the balcony with him.

"Hi, it's me," Lillian said. "What are you doing?"

Joe smiled.

"Sitting by myself watching the stars and having a glass of wine," he said.

"Sounds romantic. I have to fly to Maui tomorrow for a couple of days. Got a big job at a new condo development in Lahaina. Why don't you bring your wine over here and I can tell you all about it while we both watch the same stars."

Chapter 11

His choice of wine had been well received. And a bottle of a different red from Lillian's wine closet had been opened for comparison. Afterwards, Joe had wisely decided to spend the night there until the stars went out.

The detectives room was busy when he walked in.

"Good morning, Walt," he greeted.

"Same to you," Walt said. "I've finished with the newspaper. You can have it."

"Thanks, I'll read it later. Got an appointment with the City Attorney. Don't want to keep him waiting."

He gathered up the forms from his desk drawer, stuck them in his briefcase and left. It was a short drive to the city hall.

"You'll be seeing Assistant City Attorney Madelynn Crocker, detective," the person at the front desk told him.

"What happened to Sterling Huddleson?" Joe asked. "I've always worked with him."

"Mr. Huddleson has gone into private practice. Madelyn Crocker's office is down the hall first one on the right."

The office door was open but he knocked on it before entering.

An attractive woman perhaps in her early thirties sat behind a desk picking at her skirt.

"Have you ever seen anything like this?" she asked without looking up. "My mother sent me this stupid angora sweater that does nothing but shed. I'd written to her about how cold they keep this place. Even when it isn't all that hot outside. Please have a seat."

"Miss Crocker, I'm Detective Joe Cheo with HPD," Joe said, pulling back a chair. "I have some reports for you to look at for possible filing."

"It's worse than having a damn cat," she said, giving the skirt one last brush. "Okay, detective, let's see what you've got."

He handed her the stack of forms.

Joe took another look at her while she read. She really was attractive. Astonishingly so. He didn't notice any ring on her left finger. He wondered what her story was.

"These are very thorough and nicely written," she commented, putting down the last one. "You do them?"

"Yes, patrol had at first given the preliminary investigation reports to homicide because the battery detective was out sick. I handle auto theft and my workload was light so the lieutenant passed them on to me. Most were manini. Those you have are the ones we'd like to file."

"What did you call the others?"

"Manini. That's the Hawaiian word for a minor or small incident. Used it out of habit. My mom often spoke to me in Hawaiian. Sorry about that."

"Don't be. How do you spell it?"

Joe spelled the word and she wrote it down.

"Manini," she read aloud. "That's my second Hawaiian word to remember. I've already mastered aloha. This Kedron Olomano person looks promising."

"Yeah, he allegedly smacked a guy upside the head with a wrench. Another person who witnessed the incident called the cops. The victim's backing out. Not sure the witness is willing to stand up in court, either."

"Well, if the victim won't cooperate and the witness is iffy, that makes it all the more difficult for us. Was he badly hurt? The one who was smacked upside the head?"

"Had a bump according to the officer. Vic said he'd earlier hit his head on something else."

"Don't suppose he went to the hospital?"

"Wasn't in the report. Olomano has been in trouble before. Couldn't see his juvenile record but according to some people I talked with he was familiar with ju-vee court. Seems he's a hot head. Always bailed out by his parents and any charges quashed. They're big bucks. Dad does business in the Far East. Apparently he has a lot of influence around town."

"Nothing new about that."

"So you'll file?"

"Absolutely. Make it a misdemeanor. Don't know how far it'll go as it now stands. Certainly not to the Prosecuting Attorney. Probably send an officer to his home for a little chat. Maybe it'll give him a scare. Maybe even do him some good. I'll file the others as misdemeanors as well."

She took out a pack of cigarettes and a shot glass from her desk drawer. Joe could see there was some writing on it but all he could make out was a picture of a playing card.

"Do you mind it I smoke?"

"Not at all. Are you going to have a drink as well?"

She laughed.

"Not now but maybe later. This is just an old souvenir. I use it for an ashtray."

"Where'd you pick it up?"

"Las Vegas. Ever been there?"

"I've only been to California. Short stay while I was in the Army and before I shipped out. Las Vegas sounds like it could be fun, although I'm not much of a gambler. Were you there visiting?"

"No, I was a cocktail waitress at the FlamingoHotel and Casino at the time."

~~~

The Koolau Mountains having spent the morning babysitting a budding rainstorm handed it over to Honolulu as a downpour that afternoon. Madelyn Crocker watched the rain from the window behind her desk.

She finished a cigarette and stubbed out the butt in the shot glass. That had been only the fourth one she'd smoked all day. She was getting better at cutting down. Maybe she'd try to go cold turkey. She dumped out the ashes in the waste basket and spun the empty glass around on her desk top. Like a wheel of fortune, where would it stop? And what would it bring? Las Vegas came to mind.

She'd graduated from college and was working at the Flamingo to pick up some extra money before starting law school. She had paid for most of her undergraduate years herself, not that her family couldn't have contributed but because she wanted to be independent.

The casino waitressing jobs on the gaming floors were terrific. Players tipped well and all that was required was a good memory for drink orders and a flirty smile. The woman who'd hired her said it was also a plus if you had a great body. Well, Madelyn Crocker's body was A-plus in that department.

Toward the end of summer, Eugene Brickwood chose to shoot craps at the Flamingo instead of the Circus Circus, where he was staying for a couple of weeks with some business clients.

Eugene's dice couldn't have been hotter that night. He liked to cool off with an occasional vodka-on-the-rocks garnished with a lemon twist and Madelyn timed her arrival at the table with watch-like regularity and all her A-plus body could offer. In return, he showed his appreciation by stuffing a hundred-dollar chip down the front of her outfit each time. On the third night he asked if she'd care for a late dinner after she'd finished her shift. Normally, she would have deferred to management rules and declined. But he was cute and charming so she accepted.

A whirlwind relationship developed between them and two days before Eugene was to leave town he asked her to marry him. To both of their surprise, she agreed and they were wed in the Chapel of Hearts on the Strip. She bought a souvenir shot glass in their gift shop.

Her new husband's importing business was based in Los Angeles and he spent three to four days there each week. They decided that her tiny apartment would be adequate until he could move more of his work to Las Vegas. She was happy with that arrangement and continued her job at the Flamingo squirreling away money for law school, although the first semester had already begun without her. She told her parents that she was taking a break and would start the next semester. She didn't mention that she was now married. They never visited at her apartment, she always went to their home, so her secret was safe.

One evening when romance seemed to be in the offing, Eugene suggested they spice things up and produced a pair of hand cuffs. That encounter with dominance fanned to life a high she'd never experienced and bondage became their sexual drug of choice.

Eugene's luck ran out when he was killed in an automobile accident. Her luck changed for the better when she was named the sole beneficiary of a large life insurance policy he'd taken out. She entered law school, graduated with honors and aced the bar exams in both Nevada and California. Rather than join a law firm, which would've been expected, she applied to the Las Vegas city attorney's office and went to work there. Public service had always been part of her life. Her father worked with the city administrator's office and her mom was a police dispatcher. Later, one of her law school professors, who happened to be a good friend of the Honolulu Prosecuting Attorney, recommended her for an opening in that office. When the job offer came, she took it without a second thought. She'd had enough of Las Vegas. It was time to move on.

~~~

Joe paused on the sidewalk, which had been washed clean by the two-and-a-half inches of rainfall that had fallen earlier. He was at a loose end. There hadn't been much to do at the station after he'd returned. He'd putzed around trying to look busy until the weather cleared and then went home.

His apartment had seemed especially empty for some reason and he had almost picked up the phone to call Lillian before remembering that she was in Maui. Somehow the distance even added to the loneliness he felt. Not ready to settle in with an early dinner and an evening of boring television, he'd decided to go out. But to where? He had left that decision to his feet

And they had taken him to a familiar area of town. One he'd once covered on his beat when he was with patrol. Papa Din's was down the next block and, if he remembered correctly, it offered a pretty good bar menu. He picked up his pace.

The bar was packed but the barkeeper pointed to a single empty seat at the end. Joe ordered a beer and settled back to watch the action.

A group from the bar moved to a table, leaving four or five seats vacant. They looked as if they worked in one of the new office buildings nearby judging by the way they were dressed. Papa Din's was probably an afterwork hangout, Joe figured. The empty seats at the bar were quickly filled as more people came in, a woman taking the one next to him. Joe turned toward her.

"Hello, Detective Cheo," Madelyn Crocker smiled.

If she were surprised to see him, she certainly didn't show it. Joe, however, dropped his jaw.

"Assistant City Attorney Crocker," he sputtered.

"Oh, you remembered," she said sweetly.

"I didn't expect…," he paused and laughed. "Guess I was just surprised to run into you like this. Excuse me if I seemed a little startled."

"That's the second time today you've apologized, detective," she said. "Frankly, I was just as surprised to see you. What's the next line now? Oh, yes. Come here often?"

Joe laughed.

"Just happened to be in the neighborhood," he said.

"How coincidental. Actually, I don't live too far from here. How about you? Are we neighbors?"

"No, I live a little farther away," Joe said. "Different part of town. I was out for a walk. No particular destination. Wound up here. In fact, this used to be part of my old beat before I moved to detectives. I'd occasionally check in with the bartender. Put a face to the name, you know. Seems things might've changed some since then, however."

"Really? In what way?"

"Well, Papa Din's used to have a reputation for being a hot pickup bar. Much younger crowd then. Rowdier. Looks a little older now. More upscale. Lot of business types. Of course, that doesn't mean anything's changed when you get right down to it."

Madelynn gave him a curious smile.

"Is that what brought you here? " she asked playfully. "Looking for a hot pickup?"

"Not at all," Joe laughed. "They also had good burgers back then. I was hoping that maybe they still did."

"I don't believe that for one minute," she teased. "You're saying you walked halfway across town for a hamburger? Come on. Fess up. I won't tell anyone."

"God's honest truth," Joe said. "Pure happenstance. I'm married anyway. Don't think my wife would care much for me fooling around."

Madelyn gave him a skeptical look.

"From what I've observed with most men that little problem has never stood in the way," she said.

"Well, it does with me," Joe said seriously. "Not that I'm being priggish. Just shows that not everyone who comes in here wants to screw their brains out."

Madelyn smiled and leaned over to him. He could smell her perfume. It was intoxicating, as it was meant to be.

"I have a measured IQ of one-hundred and forty," she whispered seductively in his ear.

"Sorry, ma'am, didn't mean to ignore you," the bartender interrupted. "Little busy is all. What can I get for you?"

~~~

"Albert, I'm thinking about taking a trip."

Helen was standing before the window in the front room. The sun had set but it was still light outside. Albert was watching the news on television.

"Ronald Reagan should go back to making movies," he commented. "He could do a better job in Hollywood than he's doing in Washington. In fact, he should've bowed out after he was shot."

"Did you hear me, Albert?" Helen asked, slightly irritated.

He switched off the TV.

"I said I was going to take a trip," she repeated.

"Where?"

"Kauai."

"When did this come up?"

"I've had it on my mind for some time. I'd like to visit with some friends."

"Don't you have enough friends here?"

"That's not the point, Albert. I was born there. These are old friends I haven't seen in years. Some I grew up with. No one's getting any younger. Besides, this empty house is starting to get to me. You can understand that, can't you?"

"Of course I do. I was just surprised considering everything that's happened recently, that's all. Yes, I think that might be good for you to get away for a few days."

"I haven't decided how long I'll stay. I also may want to go over to Ni'ihau. My mother had relatives there. In fact, I spent much of my early childhood there."

"Well, don't worry. I'll take care of things here. When do you plan to leave?"

"I have to make arrangements. Maybe next week. I'll have to see."

~~~

Joe had returned from Papa Din's to find an old surfboard standing upright against the door of his apartment. It was an early foam-core design. Oddly, it looked familiar. An envelope was plastered on the fin. Inside was a note.

It read:

Joe,
This surfboard belonged to George. He was very proud of it. Don't know if you remember but I thought you might like to have it. Don't forget our little chat.
Albert

He remembered the board very well. His father would never let him use it. As for their little chat Albert mentioned, he hadn't forgotten that either.

He crumpled the note and took the board inside. He would put it out on the balcony until he decided what to do with the thing.

Suddenly, a foul mood came over him. The phone rang and he snatched it up.

"This is Joe Cheo," he growled.

"My goodness, you don't have to bite off my head," Lillian said. "Is this a bad time?"

"Didn't mean to snap," Joe apologized. "Been one of those days."

"Oh, I'm sorry. My day has been absolutely swell if that helps. In fact, I may finish this job sooner than I thought."

"Hey, that's great," Joe said, brightening somewhat. "I miss you."

"I miss you, too. What's on for tonight?"

"Early dinner and boring television."

"You should go out somewhere, Joe. Have a little fun. Be good for you."

"I'm good here."

"Well, then I won't keep you any longer. Seriously, I am meeting with the client shortly, so I really must run. Just wanted to say hello. Bye for now."

Joe held the silent phone for a moment before placing it back in its cradle.

Why didn't he talk longer? He could have told her about Papa Din's. It was a funny story.

It wasn't that he had anything to hide. Nothing happened with Madilyn Crocker. It didn't go any further. Maybe in his mind but as a former President of the United States said, that didn't count. And the irony of it all was the burger that'd brought him there in the first place turned out to be so burnt and dry that he couldn't eat it. He'd left it on the plate after one bite. You can't top that for an ending to a lousy story.

As far as Albert's surprise gift and little message went, the surfboard wasn't worth mentioning and she already knew about the job offer.

He turned on the television. A rerun of Gilligan's Island had just begun. He went to the refrigerator to rustle up something for dinner.

Chapter 12

"Joe, there's a call from a man about a car," Lola Kahemena yelled. "I'm putting it through to you."

"Was the car stolen?"

"He wasn't clear."

Looks like the day is off to a great start, Joe thought and picked up his phone. Guy's probably upset about his car.

"This is Detective Cheo with auto thefts," he said. "May I have your name, sir?"

"Bill Koki. That's K-O-K-I.'"

"And what is the make of the vehicle you are calling about, Mr. Koki."

"It's a Volkswagen Beetle."

"And when did you first notice it was missing?"

"It's not missing," Koki said. "It's right here in my shop."

Joe paused.

"Not sure I understand, Mr. Koki." he said.

"I own a body repair shop. The car came in for work a few days ago. Front-end damage but there's something about it that bothers me. I think someone from the police department should take a look."

""Do you have reason to believe the car might have been stolen?"

"The owner brought it in."

"Right. What bothers you about the damage?"

"You have to see it for yourself."

"As I told you, sir, I cover auto theft."

"That still makes you a detective, right?"

Joe paused.

"Where are you located, sir?" he asked.

"Waimea."

"Waimea? This is District 1. We're in downtown Honolulu. You want District 2. They cover Waimea."

"I called the police yesterday. They didn't say what district it was but they did promise to send an officer. So far nobody's showed up. Doesn't say much for the police department in my opinion."

Taking a nice drive around the island on a beautiful day isn't the worst idea, Joe thought. Getting out of the office for all morning wouldn't be bad, either. After all, that VW could be on a stolen list.

"What's your address, Mr. Koki?"

"Just go through Waimea on the main road to the other side. Can't miss it."

~~~

Joe maneuvered through the slower traffic on the Likiliki Highway, leaving Honolulu shrinking in the rearview mirror. Both windows were rolled down, the old car's air conditioner now nothing more than a hot breath.

He pictured the snappy red convertible he'd recently rented. He could be breezing along comfortably now with the top down and its air conditioner on arctic blast. Maybe he shouldn't worry about what the department might think.

The traffic was noisy. He switched on the radio. A sweet melody crooned from a Lahaina station in Maui and he gave his attention to the scenery.

Pipeline and Sunset passed. In the winter months, the waves would charge the beaches in mountainous blue sets but today they barely lapped at the shoreline.

Motoring through Waimea and out the other side of town, he at last came upon the auto repair shop. Bill Koke was right. He couldn't miss it.

The cinderblock building had a huge mural on one side featuring a surfer riding the face of giant wave. A sign on the front read Wipeout Repairs.

He pulled in and got out of his car. The garage door was open and he could see someone inside.

"I'm Detective Joe Cheo," he said, walking up. "Are you Mr. Koki?"

"That's right, detective. Come in."

Joe noticed a photograph thumbtacked on a bulletin board of three people as he entered the shop. One resembled Bill Koki.

"This you?" he asked, pointing to it.

"Yeah, that's me in my younger days when I had more hair," Koki chuckled. "Older fellow on the left is my dad. My kid brother's holding the long board."

Joe took a closer look at the photo.

"That's him in the painting outside," he said in surprise.

"You've got a good eye," Koki said. "Local fellow was the artist."

"I like a long board. Your brother still surf?"

"No, he died in Viet Nam."

Joe looked again at the smiling face in the photograph but now with a sad expression himself. Like so many he'd known, he thought.

"The car's in the back," Koki said, interrupting the moment.

Joe followed him to the Volkswagen which had a car cover over it.

"Cover belongs to the car," Koki said. "Thought I'd better protect its expensive paint job while it's here."

He carefully removed the car cover.

It didn't look like any Volkswagen Joe had ever seen.

The car's body was painted bright red. Highly polished motorcycle fenders fitted on the top of all four wheels. The frontend was slightly lowered. A single exhaust pipe angled up from the engine in back like it was flipping off the car behind it.

Joe walked around the car to fully take it in.

"This thing's awesome," he said.

"Real expensive toy, that's for sure," Koki said. "Engine alone probably cost five or six grand to build. Those custom aluminum fenders had to set you back, too."

"What would you do with something like this?" Joe asked.

"Have one hell of a lot of fun," Koki chuckled. "You're looking at a serious street racer."

"What's the owner like?" he asked.

"Punk kid with an attitude. Kind of put me off, frankly. Don't know how he got my name. I purposely told him we couldn't get started on his car until later. Hoped maybe he'd go away. Funny thing was he didn't complain. Thought that was kind of unusual. Most people are always in a big hurry. Want it yesterday. Anyway, the kid must have money from somewhere."

"You say he's a kid?"

"Yeah, probably seventeen or eighteen. Hard to tell these days. Could be older, I don't know. Woman followed him here in her car and took him back. Might've been his mom. Here's what I called you about."

He pointed to the right windshield post.

"Looks like that could be dried blood near the top of that A-pillar at the roofline," he said. "Got a little dent there, too. Didn't notice it at first."

Joe examined the crusty substance. There appeared to be a few strands of hair as well.

"The right front fender was bent," Koki said. "Looks like somebody tried to straightened it out. Didn't do a very good job. Got to be careful with aluminum. The hood's also knocked out of line. Could've hit around that spot first and then bounced up and off the top. Whatever it was had to have been pretty heavy to do this kind of damage."

"Might've been a big dog," Joe suggested.

"Yep, except the owner said he ran into a ditch. Now stoop down here and I'll show you something else. It's what made me first start to get suspicious."

Joe squatted and Bill Koki pointed to the underside of of the car.

"You'd expect to see some dirt caked around here if the car had run into a ditch. Everything looks washed clean. Now the other side's also fairly clean but shows road grime, which is natural. Again, looks spanking new here. I can tell this car is kept up but it's also driven. It's no garage queen. Makes me think whoever cleaned this up might've missed that little area up by the windshield. It being red, you know. That's why I decided to call you guys."

Both men got to their feet.

"Mr. Koki, you did the right thing by calling me. I'd like you to replace the cover and not let anyone near the car until you hear back from me. Also, could you possibly give me the owner's name?"

"Sure, it's on the job order."

Joe wasn't so sure about what he was doing. Bill Koki's suspicions made sense. But they also made it easy to draw wrong conclusions. And if this car has actually been involved in a criminal act, say a possible hit-and-run resulting in an injury, then he has no business going any further. He ought to call Lieutenant Ito right now. Otherwise, he's asking for trouble.

"Here you go. His name's Kedron Olomano. Lives in Diamond Head. That's what I mean about money."

Chapter 13

"He suspected the car was involved in something more serious that what the owner told him. Said he'd called the police yesterday to report it. They'd promised to send an officer but no one came."

Joe had decided to drive back to the station and report in person rather than phone. That would give him more time to think about how he should explain his involvement. He was now in Lieutenant Ito's office.

"Maybe they didn't have anyone available at the time," Ito said. "It wasn't an emergency. They couldn't drop everything to go look at a fender dent. Did he call them back?"

"He might have been trying to call them today and got put through to us by mistake," Joe said. "Or he could've simply misdialed. I don't know how he got our number. I explained to him that Waimea wasn't in our district. He was insistent somebody should look at it. In the end, I decided to just go there myself. For goodwill, if nothing else. As you pointed out, auto theft isn't too busy."

Ito let that pass.

"So how should I handle this?" Joe asked.

"You don't. It's out of our district."

"I believe Mr. Koki might be right about the accident and it should be looked into further," Joe said. "How about I follow up on what I've learned so far, in case District 2 really doesn't have anyone available like you suggested. At least, I could have forensics look at that stain. Settle it right there."

"This could all be a wild goose chase, detective," Ito grumped. "Then you will have wasted more valuable department time. Not to mention using up resources."

Ito wasn't buying it. Joe figured he had one more card to play.

"You're right, it all could be a wild goose chase," he said. "However, the car's owner may be charged with a battery that did happen in our district. So indirectly that does give us some involvement. Patrol took the preliminary report. It was part of the package you gave me to write up and present to the City Attorney for filing. She said she would file all of them, by the way."

"She?" Ito questioned. "I thought Sterling Huddleson was the CA. What happened to him?"

"He went into private practice. New person's name is Madalyn Crocker. Much better looking. Pretty smart, too. Came here from Las Vegas. Worked her way through college as a cocktail waitress."

Ito frowned.

"How do you know all of that?"

"Just came up in conversation while she read the reports."

Ito nodded.

"As far as the battery charge goes, it has nothing to do with the car in Waimea," he said sharply. "Apples and oranges, detective. Learn the difference. What I do know is this nosing around of yours could eventually be embarrassing to the department."

"Shouldn't we at least tell the homicide squad here about it?" Joe asked. "I mean if the car was involved in an accident that caused injury to someone, they'd want to know."

"Get back to work, detective. If you aren't all that busy, I'll look for some more reports that need writting up."

Joe returned to his desk.

"What was that all about?" Walt Douglas asked.

"Ito being Ito," Joe said.

He then explained in detail his morning with Bill Koki in Waimea.

"The lieutenant does have a point," Walt said. "And you believing the owner washed only one side of his car to remove evidence is pretty far out but then I've always applauded convoluted thinking."

"I try to keep an open mind," Joe smiled.

"Seriously, do you believe it really is human blood on the VW?" Walt asked. "He could have actually run into a ditch and hosed off the dirt because he's anal about keeping his fancy car spotless."

"He wasn't being finicky, he just missed seeing it," Joe countered. "Anyway, Forensics would know. There are a few strands of hair in it, too. Looked human to me. Bill Koki said the car was a serious street racer. Witness at the scene mentioned something about drag racers the night Ricky Ricola got hit."

"Where'd you get that information?"

"I talked to the lead detective covering the hit-and-run in Chinatown."

"Are you nuts? You tell Ito that?"

"He'd already stopped listening by then, so I didn't bother."

"That probably saved your ass. You know, they can't demote you much farther. Probably face the firing squad next time."

"I'll refuse to wear a blindfold," Joe said. "Actually, I think the most likely outcome is Ito will forget the whole thing. He's political and doesn't want to make waves. Has his eyes on making captain. Think he's pissed off because homicide here doesn't have a case to work hasn't had any solves lately. Other thing is the car owner's family apparently has some pull around town. Ito wouldn't want to touch that."

"How long do you think the guy at the shop will keep the car?" Walt asked.

"Hasn't started on it. Why?"

"Here's a thought. We could stick around after work and look up the hit-and-runs in the Honolulu area that were reported during the past month. Make a list of the fatals that happened before his car was brought in. Then check them out. This would all be done on our own time."

"I like that idea," Joe said.

"You have the license plate on the VW?" Walt asked.

"It's a vanity plate...K O U. I can't imagine what that would be for."

"Sounds kind of stupid. Let's run the number with motor vehicles."

~~~

Lillian's flight from Maui arrived in Honolulu during the middle of the afternoon rush hour. She was glad she hadn't driven to the airport. Better to relax in a taxi going home rather than fighting the traffic. Luck was with her and she spotted a vacant cab as soon as she exited the terminal.

"I'm going to Kahala," she told the driver.

Her trip had been more successful than she could've imagined. She couldn't wait to tell Joe. She checked her watch. Maybe he was home. If not, she'd leave a message for him to call her. She took out her cellphone and punched in his number. His machine answered.

"Hey, you," she said cheerfully. "I just got back. Taking a taxi home right now. Have some fantastic news about Maui. Give me a ring later. Bad things could be in store tonight."

Traffic had begun to thin on the freeway once they'd gotten away from the airport and soon they were approaching the Waialae Kahala area.

"My apartment building's near the hotel on Kahala Avenue," Lillian told the driver. "I'll point it out."

It was at the second intersection after turning off the freeway that a car ran the red light and broadsided the taxi. Lillian was thrown out of the rear door that flew open on impact. She never knew what hit them.

~~~

"Lot of terrible drivers out there," Walt commented. "Crying need for some driver education classes, if you ask me."

He and Joe were going through reports on one of the department computers.

"A traffic cop told me a few years back that Honolulu averaged over a thousand hit-and-runs a month," Joe said. "Most were non-injury. Guy sideswipes a car and doesn't stop. Someone trying to park and backs into the car behind him and doesn't leave a note. That sort of thing. But there were also a huge number of pedestrian fatalities. He said they rarely solved more than ten percent."

"Probably the same percentage today," Walt said. "Just a bigger number to work with."

"This month's already up to thirteen pedestrian fatalities," Joe remarked. "And we haven't even come to Ricky Ricola's."

"Yeah, second shift's already started," Walt noted. "We could be here all night. Better get a move on."

"Hey, Joe," a detective called out from across the room. "Pick up your phone. Front desk has a message. Says it's urgent."

Chapter 14

"She suffered some bruised ribs and a few scrapes," the doctor said. "There could be a hairline fracture on the L4 vertebrae. Hard to say for sure. Xray was a little vague. It'll heal by itself. Be sore for a few days. She was lucky."

"Can I see her?" Joe asked.

He was in the emergency room at the Le'ahi hospital, which was close to Kahala and had responded to the call for an ambulance.

"We've moved her to a ward on another floor where she'll stay for the night. Just for observation."

"Is there a problem?" Joe asked.

"I do have one concern," the doctor said. "She was apparently knocked unconscious in the accident, although she had come to by the time she arrived here and was able to tell us to call you at work. There' no sign of a concussion but there's always the possibility of one occurring later with any head injury. That's why we're keeping her here until the morning. I'll take you to see her now."

They went to an elevator.

"Are you a light sleeper, detective?"

"Never thought about it but now you ask I suppose I am."

"Good. You'll want to keep an ear out during the next couple of nights."

"And what am I supposed to be listening for?"

"That she's breathing. Here's the floor."

Lillian was awake and sitting upright against the pillows in bed when they entered the ward.

"Hello, Mrs. Cheo," the doctor greeted. "You have a visitor."

Joe walked over and gently kissed her on the cheek.

"How are you doing?" he asked.

"Hurt all over and then some. I don't remember a thing about what happened. They had to tell me after I got here. Isn't that strange?"

"The doctor believes you were knocked out," Joe said.

"Guess I must've been. It's all a blank. I hope the poor taxi driver is okay. Do you know, doctor?"

"He's no longer in danger," he said, avoiding her eyes. "We're letting you go home tomorrow morning, Mrs. Cheo."

Joe suspected the poor taxi driver wasn't okay.

"What time should I be here?" he asked.

"Around nine. Right now, your wife needs to get some rest."

Joe kissed Lillian.

"You heard the doctor," he said. "Get some rest. I'll see you tomorrow."

On their way back to the elevator, the doctor confirmed Joe's suspicion. The taxi driver was pronounced dead on arrival. He couldn't tell him anything about the other driver, the one who caused the accident. That person hadn't been brought to their hospital.

~~~

"My name is Joe Cheo. I work downtown."

Joe handed his police ID card to the desk officer at a station in District 7. He'd driven there from the hospital.

"I'd like to speak with someone in traffic about a fatal vehicle accident that happened here earlier today."

A detective appeared shortly after the desk officer called and led Joe back to an area where they could talk. Joe explained why he'd come.

"Sorry about your wife," Detective Terry Wong said. "Glad she wasn't hurt any worse. Not sure what I can help you with, though."

"Maybe you could just take me through the accident."

"I'll do the best I can." Wong told him. "I came in a couple of hours ago. Basically from what I understand, a car ran a red light at an intersection and plowed into the taxi your wife was riding in."

Talk about the wrong place at the wrong time, Joe thought.

"Trying to beat the light, huh?"

"My guess is he never even saw the damn light," Wong said. "The officer at the scene smelled alcohol on his breath and asked if he'd been drinking. Guy admitted that he'd had a beer. Tested him and he registered nearly twice the limit on the breathalyzer. That was at the scene. We ran a second test here and he was still about the same."

Joe's mouth tightened and the scar of his cheek became vivid.

"You still have him?" he asked.

"Yeah, he was initially arrested for the DUI," he said. "That charge has now moved up a few pegs. He'll be transported to county tomorrow. Doubt if they'll allow any bail. That's the usual case when there's a fatality involved."

"Was he injured? The doctor at Le'ahi told me he wasn't brought there."

"The bastard didn't even get a scratch," Wong said. "Isn't that a bitch? You want to go take a look at him?"

"I don't want to see him," Joe said quietly. "I want to kill him."

Wong was startled.

"Don't worry, detective," Joe told him. "Just letting off some steam. Won't hold you up any longer. It's late and I've got some things to do back at the station."

It wasn't all that late, Joe thought, getting into his car. And there wasn't anything at the station that couldn't wait. He'd earlier phoned Walt Douglass to update him on Lillian's condition. Yet he didn't feel like going home. He was still wound up.

He started the engine and drove away, heading nowhere in particular, just spooling out some time while he settled down.

To his surprise, he found himself eventually cruising around his own district. In fact, he was coming up on Papa Din's.

As he passed by, he saw Madalyn Crocker and Sterling Huddleson going into the bar arm in arm.

He decided that he'd had enough surprises for one night and headed home.

Chapter 15

"How's Lillian?"

"They should bring her down any minute now."

Joe was on the phone with Walt Douglas while waiting in the lobby at the hospital.

"I'll be nursemaiding at her place for a couple of days."

"Don't worry, Joe. I'll square it with Ito when he comes in."

"Thanks. Tell him I'll call there after we get home. Any luck on the hit-and-runs?"

"Olomano could be a player. Timing's close. Still a few more incidents to go through."

"Be great if forensics could check that blood smear before Ito blows off the whole thing," Joe said.

"Let me see what I can do," Walt said.

"One of us should give Bill Koki a call," Joe said. "Tell him we're still on the case."

"I'll do that."

"Also, fill in Detective Curtis Lam over in Chinatown. He should know what we have."

"Always room out on the limb for one more sucker, I guess," Walt said. "You realize we're both stepping way over the line. Still can't understand how or why I got mixed up in this thing. Hopefully, Lam has better sense. Maybe he can give us some."

"Hey, you," a familiar voice called out.

Joe turned to see Lillian in a wheelchair being pushed into the room.

"She's here, Walt," he said excitedly.

~~~

Tiny walked into the Mongoose Bar to find Pepe Tanaka sitting alone at a table. He was the only person in the entire place. Even the bartender was gone.

"Where is everybody?" he asked, looking around.

"On break," Pepe told him. "So this better be good."

Tiny had earlier called Pepe saying they needed to talk and that it was important they do it now. Pepe had suggested they meet at the Mongoose, a dingy little bar in an industrial park near Hilo which he and his late brother owned.

"You look like you're about to piss in your pants," Pepe said, as Tiny pulled out a chair to sit down. "Toilet's in the back, if you need to go."

"I'm all right," Tiny said. "Frank's dead. It was in the Honolulu newspaper."

"You take the Honolulu paper?" Pepe smirked.

He was purposely being cruel. He knew that Tiny couldn't read very well. At best it was at a second grade level.

"No," Tiny said, ignoring the jab.

He preferred not to provoke him. Pepe had a hot temper along with a mean streak. He'd once killed a guy in a fight. It wasn't that he felt he couldn't handle himself with Pepe. It was that they needed to talk.

"Albert told me," he said. "He read it."

"Frank was a fucking idiot."

"Albert also asked about you."

"Yeah?"

"Said he might give you a call."

"Tell him to save his dime. I don't have anything to say to him."

"He wants his stuff back."

Pepe gave him a fishy look.

"What stuff?"

"He said you'd know. He's willing to pay a reward, no questions asked."

"How much is he offering?"

~~~

"Should I carry you over the threshold?" Joe asked.

"Don't you dare even try," Lillian laughed.

They'd arrived at her apartment after a short drive from the hospital. Joe led her into the living room.

"What can I get you?" he asked.

"I'm okay. You don't have to baby me."

"Just following doctor's orders. Think I'll make a pot of coffee."

Lillian sighed.

"That'd be nice," she said. "You know where everything is."

While Joe busied himself in the kitchen, Lillian thought how lucky she was even to still be around and now have her husband here to help. She resolved to try not to complain too much.

~~~

"Detective Lam, this is Detective Walt Douglas in District 1, got a minute?"

"Sure, what's up?"

"I believe you've spoken with Detective Joe Cheo about a hit-and-run you're investigating?"

"That's right. I'm lead on that. Victim was one Ricky Ricola. Apparently he was once Cheo's snitch. You know the guy, too?"

"No, that was when Joe worked patrol. He's my partner now. Well, off and on. He asked me to call you. He would've done it himself but his wife was recently in an accident and he's home taking care of her."

"Christ, what happened? Is she all right?"

"She's fine. A car ran a light and t-boned the taxi she was in. Killed the cabby. Threw her out on pavement. The asshole that hit them was DUI."

"I heard about that accident. Didn't know it was his wife. Hope they put that driver under the jail."

"Yeah, and throw away the key while they're at it," Walt added. "Joe wanted you to know about a call he got regarding a vehicle at a repair garage the other side of Waimea. This came in after you and he talked. He believes it might have some bearing on the Ricola hit-and-run that you're handling."

"Waimea? That's in another district. Why did he get it?"

"It's kind of confusing. I think the phone lines got crossed. Anyway, the garage owner told him he'd earlier called the police and they'd promised to send an officer but nobody ever showed up. He was pissed off. Insisted that someone come see the car. Joe figured he might make a big stink about it so he went out there for public relations sake, if nothing else."

"Guess the department would appreciate that."

"Don't kid yourself."

Lam laughed.

"So here's what Joe wanted you to know," Walt said. "The car had frontend damage on one side. Owner claimed he'd run into a ditch but the garage guy wasn't buying it. There was what appeared to be dried blood in a couple of areas. The timing for your hit-and-run and when the car was brought in works. Joe thinks forensics should check it out but he's not getting any support from the brass here. Lot of politics going around. But what if this thing is righteous? Joe and I have been checking hit-and-run records. I was thinking maybe you and I could drive out there together today for a look."

"Sounds interesting. You want to pick me up?"

~~~

"Mr. Faison would like you to join him at a small gathering tonight," Lydia Ling said from the doorway of Madalyn Crocker's office.

Harlan Faison was the Prosecuting Attorney and Lydia was his secretary.

"I'd be honored," Madalyn Crocker smiled. "What sort of small gathering?"

"One with big people," Lydia sniffed. "It'll be at the Royal Hawaiian Hotel. Cocktails at seven."

"What should I wear?"

"Something suitable."

Lydia turned and left.

Madalyn was bemused. The woman had resented her from the moment they'd met. She wondered why?

The question now, however, is what should she wear that would be...suitable?

The answer was obvious.

Sexy but not too skimpy.

She had just the thing hanging in her closet.

~~~

Bill Koki removed the car cover.

"Boy, that's one weird Volkswagen," Walt Douglas said. "Never seen anything like it before."

He and Curtis Lam had arrived at the garage a few minutes earlier.

"You could buy three or four brand new Beetles for what this one must've cost," Koki said. "They make them in Mexico now. This car might've been an older model. My guess is it was built at some hotrod shop in California. Nobody around here does this kind of work. Not that much of a market for it. That dent on the top is what made me finally call the police the first time."

Lam stepped over for a closer look.

"Something's smeared on it," he said. "Could be blood, I suppose. That's not saying it's human. Or if so, it could've been the owner's. Put his hand there. Maybe it happened at another time? Do you know if he was hurt in the accident?"

"He didn't say but I didn't see any sign of injury. The other detective suggested the car might've hit a big dog,"

"Or maybe it was a low flying nene," Walt offered with a grin. "Those big geese are pretty heavy."

"There aren't any nenes left on this island," Lam told him. "Find them mostly on the other islands these days. I do like the big dog possibility, however. Could've been an Airedale coming in for a landing."

Walt laughed.

"I know it's easy to get carried away over all the possibilities but before you go any farther, stop for a moment to look at this," Koki said.

He squatted by the right front wheel. Lam joined him.

"I showed this to the other detective," he said. "Car's supposed to have run into a ditch so you'd expect to see some mud caked on the undercarriage and suspension. Would've dug into the bank. Might've damaged the suspension, too."

He ran his hand around the area.

"Spotless, right? No damage I could find, either. Now, the other side is a little grimy but no mud. Hasn't been washed. Could've smacked whatever it was harder on this side . The bent fender apparently rubbed against the tire. You can see the marks."

Lam nodded.

"I explained all this to the other detective. My feeling is he hit something else than the side of a ditch. And it bounced up against the top. Maybe it was a nene but then there're no feathers. Or could've been a flying dog but the hairs don't look right."

"Very interesting," Lam said, getting to his feet and glancing at the blood smear.

"Here's one more thing that's also interesting," Koki said. "I also told this to the other detective— that when the owner brought in the car, I said I couldn't get to it right away. That was okay with him. Then he called me late yesterday wanting to know if it was ready. Seemed all tangled up in his underwear."

"What did you tell him?" Walt asked.

"That I hadn't started on the job. He got all pissed off then and told me to forget it. Said he'd take his car somewhere else."

"Did he say when he was coming for it?" Lam asked.

"No, I feel he might've had second thoughts after he'd cooled down. Otherwise, he'd have been here and gone by now."

Lam examined the blood spot again. He thought of Ricky Ricola lying dead on the gurney in the hospital and what the ER doctor had told him about the injuries he'd sustained.

And the witness mentioning hearing two cars drag racing near the scene.

"Mr. Koki, I'd like you to put the cover back on," he said. "Be very careful. But before you do, I'd like to take a couple of pictures."

He removed an old Leica 35mm camera from his briefcase.

"That looks like a pretty expensive piece of equipment," Walt commented.

"My dad got it in Germany after the war," Lam said. "He was an occupation soldier. I use it a lot for documentation at the scene. Sometimes it helps to have your own stuff."

He snapped a few shots from different angles.

"I think there's evidence that this vehicle was involved in a crime," he said. "What do you say, Detective Douglas?"

"I agree," Walt nodded "We should have it towed to the impound yard for forensics to examine it."

"Hold on a minute," Koki jumped in. "I don't want to get sued. This guy comes from money. Probably has a whole string of lawyers."

"You have nothing to worry about, sir," Lam said. "If the owner shows up before we leave, we'll be more than happy to explain the situation to him. Otherwise, he can phone us."

He handed him his card.

"Call me any time," he said. "And I'll need a statement from you detailing the damage to the car and what the owner said had caused it."

"Okay if I use your office phone, Mr. Koki?" Walt asked, also giving him his own card. "My cellphone breaks up a little out here."

"I should make the call for impound, Walt," Lam said. "I'm lead should anyone have a question."

"Good thinking," Walt agreed. "Joe and I aren't officially on this. So better to keep us in the shadows."

They waited another two hours for the tow truck to arrive. Kedron Olomano hadn't come for his car. Bill Koki closed up for the night.

Chapter 16

The taxi pulled up and stopped at the entrance of the Royal Hawaiian Hotel. A doorman immediately rushed over and opened the passenger door. Madalyn Crocker gracefully slipped out of the rear seat.

She looked stunning in a fitted red dress with a modestly revealing bust line and a single slit running up from the hem to just above the knee. A string of small pearls circled her neck. Two small gold bangles dangled on her left wrist. Her thick brunette hair fell loose on her shoulders. She wore her makeup sparingly.

"Welcome to the Royal Hawaiian," the doorman greeted. "Any luggage, ma'am?"

"No, I won't be staying."

She stood for a moment taking in the magnificent pink building. She could see why it was called the Pink Palace.

The doorman led her to the lobby.

Inside she could see nothing concerning the party. No poster announcing the event. No one sitting at a table handing out name tags. She'd have to ask at the front desk. Then she realized she hadn't bothered to find out who was throwing the damn thing. A young man dressed in a flowered Aloha shirt and wearing a lei around his neck approached her.

"Good evening, Ms. Crocker," he said. "My name is Frederick Mahoe. May l escort you to the Garden Suite."

He offered her his arm.

"How did you recognize me?" she asked.

"I was given an excellent description. We'll take the elevator to the second floor."

"The garden is on the second floor?"

"The suite has a garden view."

They emerged from the elevator and walked down a short hall to the suite. Madalyn could hear noisy chatter and laughter coming from inside.

A man dressed exactly as Frederick, down to the identical lei around his neck, stood at the entrance.

"Good evening, Ms. Crocker," he greeted and opened the door.

The chattering noise immediately swelled. Amazing, she thought, noticing that for a small gathering the room was quite crowded. She stepped in.

"Madalyn," Harlan Faison shouted, spotting her and coming over.

"Who are all these people?" she whispered.

"Politicians, lawyers, business types, wannabes, take your pick. I'll introduce you to our host, Louis Olomano."

He pointed to a group of people standing by a large window overlooking the garden.

"The little round man in the powder-blue suit is Olomano," he said. "The Asian fellow is who he's throwing this blast for. That's Sterling Huddleson standing next to him. Funny, I hadn't noticed Sterling until now. Maybe he just arrived, too."

Madalyn had already recognized Huddleson. She didn't mention it, however.

"I don't know who the other person is," Faison said. "Probably some Olomano ass-kisser."

They made their way across the room.

"Mr. Olomano, I'd like you to meet Madalyn Crocker," Faison said. "She's our new Assistant City Attorney."

Olomano gave her an appraising look, actually more of a sizing up.

Madalyn returned it with a disdainful look.

"A pleasure to meet you, Ms. Crocker," he said, offering a limp hand.

"Madalyn recently came to us from Nevada where she worked in the Las Vegas city attorney's office," Faison said.

"Are you originally from Las Vegas, Ms. Crocker?" Olomano asked, showing a little more interest.

"My home town," Madalyn answered sweetly.

"So many casinos there," Olomano said.

"Bless them all," Madalyn smiled sweetly. "They paid my way through college."

Olomano turned to the Asian man in the group and said something. She couldn't understand a word.

"And may I introduce our guest of honor, Ms. Crocker," Olomano said, turning his attention back to her. "This is Mr. Kim Heng."

Heng grinned and bowed. Madalyn noticed that he seemed fascinated by the slit in her dress. Eye-smacked, in fact.

"Mr. Heng is visiting from Macau and is not very fluent in English," Olomano explained. "I happen to speak Mandarin, as do most of the people in China. I mentioned to him that you're with the city attorney's office and had worked in the same position in Las Vegas before coming here. He's very impressed."

"We've also been impressed by her," Faison said proudly. "Sterling Hudson was our loss and Madalyn is our gain."

Huddleson gave him a bored smile.

"Good to see you, Sterling," Faison said, turning to him.

"Nice seeing you, Harlan," Huddleson sniffed.

"Jennifer's not here tonight?" Faison asked.

"No, unfortunately my wife is out of town," he explained smoothly. "Now, if everyone will excuse me, there's someone I must see."

Madalyn slipped him a sly wink before he left.

"Hi, I'm Brook Peters," the other person said, thrusting out his hand to her. "I'm with the mayor's office in Hilo."

"Mr. Peters is representing the mayor, who unfortunately couldn't attend our gathering tonight," Olomano said.

"He's down with a bug that's going around," Peters volunteered. "A friend of his, Albert Cheo, who also knows Mr. Olomano, was supposed to come with him. That was a disappointment to both of them."

Madalyn wondered if the mayor's friend was any relation to Joe Cheo. Then that reminded her that he'd mentioned Olomano was the father of the person he'd asked her to file on. She saw that Olomano's face had hardened.

"I hope I'm not being rude but my curiosity is killing me, Mr. Olomano," she said. "May I ask what does Mr. Heng do?"

Olomano delayed a moment before answering.

"He's with the syndicate in Macau which was formed by business men both in Macau and Hong Kong to promote the government gambling industry," he said. "Very important to their economy. I imagine you have a similar association in Las Vegas."

"Yes, they're called the mob," she said.

Faison swallowed almost audibly to stifle a laugh.

"Well, we must move about the room," Olomano said coolly. "Please excuse us. Very nice meeting you, Ms. Crocker."

He whispered something to Heng who nodded and smiled broadly again at Madalyn before leaving.

"What is this so-called little gathering really all about?" she asked Faison.

"I can't believe what you just said to Olomano," he said. "The mob, that was beautiful."

"He deserved it," Madalyn said. "So tell me why all the glitter tonight?"

"Legalized gambling might pass this year in the legislature," he said. "It's still a long shot but several representatives are pushing for a bill."

"So where does China come in?" she asked.

"Macau supports itself almost entirely on gambling. They tax the hell out of it. Some people believe Macau might be a good model for Hawaii to follow if the law's approved. Not so much for the gambling houses Macau runs but for their casino industry. Casinos would be restricted to the hotels here. Easier to regulate that way. Prevent the money from being misled. At least, that's the thinking. My thinking is good luck with that. Same goes with even getting the bill on the docket. There's also one other small detail that's easy to overlook but can come back to bite you. Macau's dependency on gambling isn't built on solid ground. It grows or falls with the prosperity of other countries' economies. Get a decline in any one and those people stop coming to throw away their money. Others can quickly follow."

"So this meet-and-greet is just a hype for getting backers to approve gambling in Hawaii. And your role?"

"Don't have one. I'm just an observer on behalf of the governor. Which is why I wanted you to come, as well."

"I do have one more question," Madalyn said. "What's Olomano's connection with this?"

"He does business in China. Has trade licenses with them. Knows lots of important people over there with deep pockets and the same around here."

"Well, you should know this then. I recently filed a misdemeanor report on his son."

"Actually, I do know that," he said. "Elliot Farce quashed it."

Madalyn looked at him stunned.

"Who did that?" she asked.

"Judge Elliot Farge," Faison said. "Big name in the district court. Been there forever."

"That filing was based on a solid police report," Madalyn said angrily. "I realize it's not a big deal but there's the principle of the thing. Principles still exist, don't they?"

"I've no doubt that they do. Nor that Judge Farge's being an old buddy of Louis Olomano had anything to do with his decision."

Madalyn turned away.

"I think you should buy me a drink," she said.

~~~

"Lillian's gone to bed," Joe said. "Probably hit the sack myself soon, although it's not that late. This nursing job's tougher than I thought. Takes it out of you, man."

"She doing okay?" Walt Douglas asked.

They were on the phone. Douglas had called to fill in Joe on what had happened at Bill Koki's.

"Her back's causing her some pain," Joe said. "Difficult getting to her feet. She gives me a shout when she needs help."

"She yells, you jump, huh?"

"Yeah, but I really don't mind," Joe said. "I kind of enjoy being here for her. Have to say Lieutenant Ito was pretty understanding when I talked with him. Said to take as much time as I need."

"Probably just happy not having to put up with you for awhile," Walt chuckled.

"I'm sure that somehow he'll hold this over me later," Joe said. "Anyway, Kedron Olmano is looking better and better as suspect number one. Be interesting to see what forensics finds out. Don't know if they can ID the individual that the blood belongs to. DNA can be iffy if they don't have a ton of sample to test. But they should be able to tell if it's human."

"You work with what you have," Walt agreed. "Like to be at the garage when the jerk comes for his car and finds out we have it."

"Funny how he suddenly wants it back," Joe said. "The assistant city attorney filed that misdemeanor on him. Maybe he's been notified by the court and has panicked about the car. Like he has other plans now. Such as getting rid of it for good."

"Wonder if we should pay him a visit?" Walt asked. "Put a little pressure on him."

"You said Lam ordered the impound. Actually, it's his case. Might be better if we stayed out."

"Yeah, but you were first to see the car. That gives us some dibs."

"Ask Lam what he wants to do about us. I'm good with anything."

~~~

"If it was up to me, I'd put a couple or three casinos on every damn island," Josh Hamuri growled and held up a hand to hail the cocktail server. She quickly came over and he ordered a dirty martini on-the-rocks from the bar.

"You want anything? he asked Madalyn Crocker.

Faison had excused himself to go speak with another guest.

"No, thanks," she said.

Hamuri was an aide in the mayor's office in Maui. He was at the party to represent the county, which also consists of Kahoolawe, Lanai and Molokai. An urgent matter had suddenly cropped up to prevent his honor from attending.

Madalyn realized that seemed to be the same situation with the mayors on the other islands. That urgent-matter bug must be getting around.

Hamuri's drink came.

"We depend big time on tourism," he said, taking a sip. "It pays the rent. Yeah, there are other industries but tourism is number one."

"I should think the beauty of the island would be enough to attract people," Madalyn Crocker said.

"As long as everything's going okay in the overall economy," Hamuri said, slightly slurring. "But soon's that starts slowing down all bets are off. Already starting to happen in some states is what I read . People tightening their belts. Putting off coming to Paradise. Got more important things to worry about. Couple of hotels are on the market in Maui right now. I hear some more on the Big Island might be looking for buyers."

"So gambling would offer the islands some insurance against, say, a recession developing," Madalyn said.

"Absolutely. People would still come here, maybe not as often but then, maybe more so. The hotels are on their hands and knees begging the legislature to pass the bill. But then there are the local politics to consider. Not everyone is on board. Worried about crime. Families going into debt. Losing their houses. That's why none of the mayors showed up here tonight. Covering their butts for the next election depending on which way the economic wind blows. And you've got the churches, too. They can rile up the voters like you can't believe."

"Then it's not a sure bet, as it were, that the legislators will even agree on initiating a bill," Madalyn said, "much less putting it up for a vote."

"I think we'll get it done. And once the money starts rolling in, all this bullshit will be long forgotten."

A woman serving hors d'oeuvres and wearing a lovely sarong identical to that the woman working on the other side of the room slowly walked past.

"Anything you would like?" she said, presenting the tray.

Hamuri raked off a handful and gave her a lecherous look.

~~~

"Bathroom!"

"What?"

"I have to go to the bathroom," Lillian said.

"Oh, yeah, sure," Joe said, sitting up in bed and shaking off his sleepiness. "Give me a second."

He fumbled for the bedside lamp and switched it on.

"Oh, that's so bright," Lilian complained, squinting.
"Can't see otherwise," Joe said. "Might trip over something."
He carefully guided her to the bathroom.
"Thank you," she said. "I feel so bad you have to do this."
"All in the job."
And no, he really didn't mind one bit.

Chapter 17

The party had thinned out somewhat but there were still enough hangers-on to keep things going.

Louis Olomano and Kim Heng had stopped by to thank Madalyn and Faison for coming before leaving themselves. Heng had been especially effusive with Madalyn. She suspected had he stuck around any longer he might've even have made a pass at her. For all she knew, he'd been making one then but didn't know how to follow up.

"You want another drink?" Faison asked.

"Maybe a glass of champagne," Madalyn said. "I think they're still pouring the good stuff."

"I'll get us both one" Faison offered and left for the bar.

Madalyn looked around the room. Her eye fell on a man she could swear she'd seen before. It had to have been some time ago, though. Possibly while she was in law school and maybe even before that. Yes, most likely then, and even more probably at the Flamingo. But for the life of her she couldn't put a name to him. Yet she felt she ought to. Made the mystery even more intriguing.

She was about ready to walk over and ask him who he was when Faison returned.

"Got there just in time," he said. "They're starting to close the bar."

"Thank you," Madalyn smiled, sipping her champagne.

She looked back across the room. The man was gone.

"That's odd," she said, puzzled. "I just saw someone over there I thought I recognized but now he's disappeared."

"Something we might consider doing soon," Faison said. "Getting pretty late. Who was the guy?"

"That's just it. I can't remember his name. But he looked familiar. I was thinking he might've been someone from where I used to work. Not important. It was just funny."

A flash of lightning startled everyone. Thunder rumbled and rain began to splatter on the windows. Within seconds it'd become a downpour.

"Now I'll be forever driving home," Faison groaned.

"Leave your car here," Madalyn said. "I'm taking a taxi. We can share."

Several miles away at the police impound yard the storm was well underway.

~~~

"Good morning," Joe said, pulling back the bedcovers. "Time to rise and shine."

Lillian grunted and tugged the covers under her chin.

"That was some storm last night," Joe said, getting out of bed. "How are you feeling?"

"Actually, I feel pretty good," Lillian said with a yawn. "A storm? I didn't hear a thing."

"Coming down like cats and dogs, yowling and howling half the night. Need some help standing up?"

"No, I'd like to try it on my own."

She sat on the side of the bed for a moment to get her bearings and then got to her feet.

"There!"

She grinned and took a few tentative steps.

"See that?"

"Careful," Joe cautioned, reaching to steady her.

"You know, I think I can make it to the bathroom by myself," she said.

"I'll follow along just in case."

"All right, but hands off," she laughed. "I'm tired of being treated like an invalid."

"How about I go fix us breakfast then?" Joe said.

~~~

"What do you mean they left it outside?" Walt Douglas asked incredulously. "Are you saying the car stayed out in that fucking rain all night?"

He was at his desk and on the phone with Curtis Lam, who had called him from the impound yard.

"Yeah," Lam said. "Apparently the garage was full. We should've followed the98 damn truck there. Had them make room inside for it."

"Anything left for forensics or was it all washed off?" Walt asked.

"We might get a break," Lam said. "The cover was still on it. Gave some protection. We've moved the car into the garage now. The tech is running some tests but said the sample could be compromised. Might give a false reading."

"Did he say when he'd know something?"

"Still working. He complained that we should've tested it at the scene. Told him we're trying to find out if the car was even at the scene. Don't know how he felt about that."

"All we can do is keep our fingers crossed," Walt said. "Too much to hope that he could type it, I guess."

"That'd take a miracle with this guy," Lam said. "You want to come out?"

"Yeah, nothing much going on here. I'll call Joe and let him know what's up."

~ ~ ~

Kedron Olomano had slept late. When he'd finally awakened and had gotten out of bed, he'd discovered the house was empty. Then he'd remembered that his mom had her stupid women's club meeting this morning, which killed any chance of her driving him to get his car.

He needed to have it before his dad returned from wherever the hell he'd gone. He'd already made a big deal about that dumb court thing before he left. He never listened to his side. He didn't even see him half the time for crap's sake.

His story about what happened to the car was okay with his mom. She was cool with everything. She and his dad never talked anyway.

But his dad would go ballistic about the insurance going up. Not wonder if he'd been hurt or anything like that. It's always the same old bullshit.

He can find somebody else to bang out the fender. His mom will pay for it and his dad will never know.

The other thing was his dad's dorky station wagon that he'd been driving was embarrassing to be seen in. He'd better fill up the gas tank, though. Otherwise, there'll be a shitstorm about that.

Maybe the old fart at the repair shop would bring his car to the house, if he asked nice. He went to the kitchen, grabbed a bottle of milk out of the refrigerator, took a swig and picked up the wall phone and dialed. Just as it began to ring, he heard someone come in the front door. Probably the maid. This was her day. Shit, he was bare-ass naked.

"Wipeout Repairs," a voice answered. "This is Bill Koki."

"Hello, Mr. Koki," he said politely. "It's Kedron Olomano. I can't get there today to pick up my car. Could you have someone bring it here? I live in Diamond Head. I'll pay you."

"Your car's no longer here, Kedron. The police impounded it last night. You'll have to talk with them about returning it. Aloha."

The dial tone followed.

Kedron stood dumbfounded.

"Oh, my goodness!" the maid giggled from the kitchen doorway.

He covered himself with his hands and hurriedly brushed past her.

Chapter 18

"Glad you had time to see me, Louis," Albert said.

Louis Olomano and Kim Heng were at the old Hukilau Hotel in Hilo. They'd arrived in a chartered helicopter from Honolulu earlier that morning. Albert had called Olomano the day before and had learned that he'd be in Hilo. He'd asked if they could meet. Now they were all seated in the hotel garden.

"Time's precious," Olomano said testily. "I prefer not to waste it."

He would also prefer that Albert not address him by his first name. He was a stickler for formality. And they certainly weren't close friends, for that matter.

"Are you making an offer on the hotel?" Albert asked breezily.

"Not today, Mr. Cheo. There's another property in Maui I want to see first."

Albert leaned back and crossed his arms, a look of concern on his face.

"I wouldn't wait too long, if I were you, Louis," he cautioned. "As you no doubt know the Hukilau comes with a lot of history. Been here a long time. Very famous. People from all over have heard about the Hukilau. Often it's difficult to get a booking they're so busy. It would be a very good investment in my opinion."

"Thank you, Mr. Cheo," Olomano said patiently, "but I'm not investing in history. I'm investing in the future, as will the partners in this venture. Mr. Heng will serve as a silent partner to help guarantee that future."

Albert remained silent himself.

"Mr. Heng holds an important position in the Macau gambling industry," Olomano explained. "He will act as an advisor. His experience could also help the state get off on the right foot once the law is passed. I've been in touch with some of the legislators regarding that and they're very enthusiastic."

"And how is that looking, Louis?" Albert asked.

"What, the law passing?" Olomano scoffed. "I don't think there's any doubt that it will pass, Mr. Cheo. Now, as to the partnership. There will be ten partners who will equally share seventy-five percent of the annual income. The remaining twenty-five percent will go toward funding future investments. The buy-in is one million dollars. That will give us enough cash to cover initial financing. Possibly more operating money, as well, depending on the source of the loan. I'm also looking into that, as you would expect."

Albert gave a little whistle.

"One million dollars," he said. "Last time we talked, it was five hundred thousand."

"As with any investment, the expected return determines the price, Mr. Cheo. Also, as I would imagine, you had determined that before making your recent pharmaceutical investment. I won't be so rude as to ask how that is going."

The slimy little bastard probably knows full well how it's going, Albert thought to himself. He's more connected than he'd realized. He'll have to keep that in mind.

"How soon do you need the money?" he asked.

"I wouldn't wait too long if I were you."

~~~

Walt Douglas had swung by Lillian's apartment to pick up Joe on the way to the impound yard. She had insisted that he go with Douglas. Some time to herself would be a welcomed relief. And although Joe had no problem with staying behind, he did appreciated the opportunity to get out of the house and back on the job even if just for a little while. Detective Lam and the forensics tech had been waiting for them inside the yard's garage.

"This is Chad Markley," Lam said, introducing the technician. "Tell them what you've got."

Markley gave a modest smile.

"The smear near the top of the windshield was the only blood sample I tested. I did look at the front of the car around the fender and hood and also beneath it even though that whole area had been washed. I didn't see anything there that looked promising. However, I can report with some certainty that the blood is human. I also suspect the hairs came from the same source."

"With some certainty?" Joe questioned.

"Ninety percent sure. I don't think you can get any closer than that."

"That's in the ballpark," Joe said."Could you type it?"

"It is type B. Ten percent of the population has type B. DNA is what you need to absolutely point a finger. We can look for that but I wouldn't hold my breath. There's simply not enough material."

"So right now we only have circumstantial evidence," Lam said. "Won't hold up in court but we can build on it."

"Be nice if Olomano has type B," Joe said.

"Be a big help," Lam agreed. "Another possibility is it belongs to someone who was with him. Bill Koki said Olomano didn't appear to have been injured."

"Wonder if he ever came for his car," Walt chuckled. "Bet he got a big surprise."

"Let's find out," Lam said.

He picked up the office phone and dialed.

"Wipeout Repairs," Bill Koki answered. "This is Bill."

""Hello, Mr. Koki, this is Detective Curtis Lam. Wanted you to know that we're keeping the Volkswagen a little longer. Anything from the owner?"

Koki laughed.

"He called me this morning," he said. "Real polite this time. Said he couldn't get to the shop and asked if I could deliver it to his home. Told him I no longer had his car. The police took it and he'd have to talk with you."

"How did that go down?" Lam asked, shooting a quick glance at the others.

"Don't know. I hung up."

Lam grinned.

"Thank you, sir. Aloha."

"What did he say?" Joe asked.

"Said the owner knows we have his car. He called this morning."

"That must've rattled his cage," Walt said. "I'd thought earlier that we should ask him to come in for a talk. Remember me saying that, Joe? Maybe we should do that now. Explain that we're trying to clear up a matter involving a car like his."

"Yeah, he might fall for that," Lam agreed. "Lean on him a little. We can tell him anything we want as long as we don't say it's an actual fact. He might confess. It's happened before."

"Or he might bring a lawyer," Joe said. "Still, it'd throw a scare at him."

"You make the phone call, Curtis," Walt suggested. "It's your case. Have him come in to see you. Our department's tin-hat boss isn't be very supportive of any interoffice cooperation. He'd raise a stink about our little task force."

"Walt has a point," Joe said. "I passed on my feelings about the coincidence of Ricola and Lofume living in the same apartment building and the possibility of a connection between them to our homicide squad. See if they thought the detectives at the station handling Lofume would be interested in knowing. They said forget about it, probably nothing more than a coincidence. We stand a better chance of getting something done if we keep low. Especially where my being involved is concerned."

"Joe's right about that," Walt said.

"Fine with me," Lam said. "Don't think our department lieutenant would have a problem. I'll call Olomano when I get back to the station. Try to set up a time. Let you know soon as I find out. Then you can come and watch the show."

~ ~ ~

"What's the license number again?" the man asked.

Kedron Olomano was on the phone with the impound yard. He'd first called the police station and been directed to call 911 where HPD had given him the yard's location and phone number.

He had put on some clothes after his encounter with the maid but had remained in his room for the entire time she was there. When she'd finally finished cleaning and had left the house, he'd gone downstairs to begin calling about his car.

"K...O...U," Kedron slowly spelled out, thinking this guy must be an idiot. "It's all letters. No numbers. Just letter K, O and U. The car's a red Volkswagen. Kind of customized."

"That's the license, three letters? You must know somebody to get a short plate like that. Yeah, that VW is here. Pretty cool looking drive."

Kedron felt some relief. At least the idiot had his car. He still didn't understand why the police had towed it away. Maybe it had something to do with the parking tickets he hadn't paid. But how did they know his car was at garage? Did that dumbass Bill Koki call them for some reason?.

"Did they say why it was towed?"

"Nope, you'll have to ask them."

"How much will it cost to get it out?"

"The towing charge would normally be fifty-five bucks plus three dollars for each mile. In your case, that'd come to an even hundred. But there's a hold on that car."

"What's a hold mean?'

"It means that car's going nowhere until the police release it. You'll have to talk with the detective that ordered the hold. Wait a minute and I'll get his name."

Kedron hung up without waiting.

This screws up everything, he thought. He didn't want to talk to any dickhead cop. He had an extra ignition key. What if he just went there and got his car? Probably a stupid fence around the place and a locked gate. His dad will shit a brick now.

The telephone rang, startling him.

"Who is this?" he asked abruptly.

"Hello, I'm Detective Curtis Lam with the Honolulu Police Department. Is this the Olomano residence?"

His mom came in the front door at that moment.

"Hello, dear," she called out sweetly. "Who's that on the phone?"

Chapter 19

Lam had explained on the phone that a car similar to the Volkswagen had been involved in an accident and they needed him to come in and help clear up some details. Kedron sugarcoated the story to his mom and she had driven him to the police station. He'd assumed that he would be getting his car back and she could then take him to the impound yard.

The desk officer had sent word to detectives that they'd arrived and were waiting in the lobby. Lam went out to meet them.

"I'm afraid you'll have to remain here, Mrs. Olomano," he said.

"Why can't I come with him?" she asked, puzzled.

"It's just the rules, ma'am," Lam smiled. "If you need anything, the desk officer will be happy to get it for you. This shouldn't take long."

Lam led Kedron back to an interview room.

"Have a seat, son," Lam said. "I'll be right back. Need anything? Soft drink, coffee, water?"

"Can I get a Coke?"

"Sure."

Lam left, closing the door behind him. Kedron heard the lock click. Everything was suddenly quiet. He was seated behind a desk facing an empty chair on the other side. Another chair stood against the wall. He looked around the tiny room. He noticed there was no wall switch for the bright overhead light. All the walls were completely bare. It was if he were sealed inside a box. Uneasiness began to creep over him.

"How's the picture?" Lam asked, entering the adjoining room .

Walt Douglas and Joe Cheo were watching a live video feed of the interview room. They'd come to the station after Lam had called.

"Great," Walt said. "Sound is good, too. Think he might be starting to sweat. Seems a little anxious."

"He's going to stretch that shirt out of shape if he isn't careful," Joe said.

Kedron had stuck both arms under the front of his teeshirt and sat hunched over.

"He wouldn't be in this jam if he'd come forward in the first place," Walt said.

"I'll let him stew a few more minutes," Lam shrugged. "He wants a Coke. Have to see what's in the machine."

"Might want something stronger after this," Walt said.

"I heard they're thinking of changing the drinking age to twenty-one," Joe put in. "Afraid he'll have to stick with the Coke awhile longer."

"Well, he'll be legal when he gets out," Walt grinned.

"Don't count your chickens," Lam told him.

"You need change for the machine?" Joe asked.

~~~

"Where the hell are Douglas and Cheo?" Ito asked, storming into the detectives room. He'd been meeting with the captain all morning.

"I'm afraid Detective Cheo is still on compassionate leave to care for his wife who was injured in an accident, as you remember," Lola Kahmena told him. "Detective Douglas didn't say where he was going."

"I thought that leave was over," Ito grumbled. "Doesn't Douglas know he's supposed to sign out when he leaves? Have him see me as soon as he gets back."

He went into his office and shut the door.

~~~

"You're a lucky guy, Kedron," Lam smiled, entering the interview room. "This was the last Coke in the machine."

He pulled out his chair and sat down.

"Thank you again for coming in today," he said, opening his briefcase and removing a folder. "As I told you, we just need to clear up a few things concerning your car."

"Am I going to get my car back today?"

"Possibly. Let's talk about your car for a moment."

He placed a photograph of the VW on the table. It'd been taken at the impound yard.

"That's one mean looking machine. Must be a blast to drive, huh?"

Kedron grinned.

"How fast will it go?"

"Don't know."

"Oh, sure you don't," Lam chuckled good naturedly. "C'mon, be honest. I won't give you a speeding ticket. Will it do a hundred?"

"Yeah," he demurred.

"Probably do that in second gear," Lam laughed. "Bet it's quick off the line in a drag race. A real killer between stoplights, right?"

He paused, looking for a tell but saw nothing.

"Ever let someone else drive your car...dad?...mom?" he asked.

Kedron sneered.

"My dad drives some kind of old station wagon," he said. "He wouldn't even get in my car. Mom doesn't know how to drive a stick shift."

"What about your friends?"

"No way."

"Don't blame you. So you're the only wheelman," he said, pulling out a piece of paper and placing it on the desk. "This is an estimate for some repairs on your car at a shop over in Waimea. What happened?"

Kedron hesitated.

"Kind of expensive," Lam continued. "What did you hit?"

"I ran into a ditch."

"Gosh, were you hurt?"

"No."

"Anyone with you?"

"I was by myself."

Lam grunted.

"Where was that ditch?"

"I don't remember. I wasn't paying attention, just cruising around."

"Myself in a car like this, I'd cruise Waikiki," Lam said. "No ditches there. Just girls. Or maybe say… over in Chinatown? Lot of action there."

He paused and looked again for a tell at that last comment but once more saw nothing.

"Let's hold it here for a moment," he said, getting to his feet. "I'll be right back."

He left the room.

The uneasiness remained there with Kedron.

~~~

Kedron's mom had begun to worry. She hadn't heard anything back since he was led away by the detective. She looked at her watch. Not all that much time had passed. Still, why were they being so secretive? She didn't like it.

"Is there a telephone here I can use?" she asked the desk officer. "I have to call someone."

"Pay phone out there where you came in, ma'am," he said, pointing at the entrance.

She thanked the officer and fumbled through her purse for some change. She remembered the number she needed though she'd never called it before. That was an odd gift she'd had all of her life. A telephone number immediately became indelibly printed in her mind the first time she heard it. She went to the phone and dialed.

"Huddleson Law Firm," the receptionist answered.

"Hello, this is Teresa Olomano. May I speak with Sterling?"

~ ~ ~

"Think it's time to raise the stakes," Lam said. "See where it takes us."

He was at the playback area with Walt and Joe.

"Ask him some more about that so-called ditch," Joe said. "Seemed like he made it up."

"How about we double team him," Walt suggested. "I'll play bad cop."

"Hey, why should you get all the fun?" Joe protested. "Let me do it."

"You're too scary," Walt told him. "Besides you're supposed to be home taking care of Lillian. We have to keep a low profile, remember? Especially you."

"Let's go, Walt," Lam said.

The two detectives left Joe with the video and headed for the interview room. Kedron had removed his arms from under his shirt when they entered and was sitting calmly with his hands in his lap.

"This is Detective Douglas," Lam said. "He will be joining us."

Walt scowled at Kedron without saying anything and pulled the extra chair over to the table. He sat down facing him.

"I believe we were talking about your running into that ditch," Lam began after seating himself. "How fast were you going?"

Kedron shrugged.

"Don't remember. Not real fast."

Walt cleared his throat and looked to one side.

"Well, don't worry about that," Lam smiled. "Like I said before, we aren't going to give you a speeding ticket. What kind of ditch was it? Deep? Shallow?"

"I don't know. Just a ditch."

"Okay, let's say it was a regular drainage ditch about yay deep. Kind you see around the more rural parts."

Lam spread his arms a couple of feet apart to illustrate the depth.

"Yeah, that looks about right."

"And the ditch was dug in the ground off the the side of the road. That's were they usually are."

"Uh-huh."

"Well, you see, that's just what's puzzling me, Kedron. We've had some rain lately all over the island and I would expect that ditch would've been muddy. Might've even had some water in it. Wouldn't you agree, Detective Douglas?"

Walt nodded.

"Yet, your car was absolutely clean. Not a speck of mud anywhere. See what I'm getting at? Help me out here."

Kedron worked his mouth slightly.

"I washed it off when I got home so I could see how much it'd been damaged," he said.

"That certainly would be one way to explain it," Lam nodded. "Detective Douglas, you have anything you'd like to ask?"

Walt leaned back in his chair.

"I saw your car at the repair shop," he said. "You must've hit that ditch pretty hard. Fender bent back. Some body damage. It's a wonder you weren't hurt."

Kedron shrugged.

"When you were examining the damage after the accident, was anything broken off that had a sharp edge that could've cut you?"

Kedron shook his head.

"Good. Glad for that. I noticed your license plate. K...O... U. What's it mean?"

"It means the car," Kedron said. "Knock out you. Get it?"

"That's very clever," Walt said. "I figured the first two letters might be your initials. Wasn't sure about the last one. But yeah, I get it now. Fits that car perfectly. Real creative of you."

Kedron smiled.

"Three little letters," Walt went on. "Neat plate like that would be easy to remember, too."

He leaned forward in his seat and looked directly at Kedron.

"So what would you say if I told you somebody did remember seeing that very license plate recently in Chinatown? Not somewhere out in the country but here in Chinatown."

The smile faded on Kedron's face.

"And what would you say if I told you that person was a witness to a hit-and-run that recently happened there?"

Kedron's expression became impassive.

"Finally, what if I told you the victim in that accident died?"

He leaned back in his chair and let that hang in the air.

"Do you have anything to tell us, Kedron?" Lam asked quietly.

A knock on the door interrupted.

"Shit," Lam muttered, getting up and opening it.

Sterling Huddleson stood there with a uniformed officer.

Chapter 20

A million dollars in cold cash wasn't something you'd normally keep around the house. Albert realized his chances of raising that much money on short notice fell somewhere between slim and none. He'd be searching for loose change under the sofa cushions where he now sat in the living room before it was over.

He wouldn't be in this predicament had he been able to sell the drugs. Louis Olomano's doubling the price wouldn't have mattered. Greedy little bastard. He could've paid twice that.

Olomano probably knew about everything. He wasn't blind to the drug trafficking here. Probably why he decided to stick it to him.

He wasn't completely broke. But cash flow was slow at the moment. And losing that seventy five thousand was a setback. He had some reserve but he didn't want to touch that if he could avoid it.

He hadn't made up his mind what to do about Pepe Tanaka. That was a dilemma. He felt certain that Pepe was behind stealing the drugs. Cooked it up with Frank Lofume, who got himself killed in the process. He wondered if anyone else was involved? That was a strong possibility he should keep it in mind.

But why aren't the the drugs on the street? Maybe Pepe doesn't know the right people to get them to the dealers. That could be an opportunity. He could offer to put him in touch with his middlemen. They were waiting. He'd just take a cut. That would be better than nothing, which was what he now had. He could even sweeten the deal by offering him a piece of his share of the casino business. Things could change in the future. Nothing's forever. And he could make sure it wasn't. All this would depend on Pepe's actually having the drugs or access to them. Which is questionable.

On the other hand, he could forget about the drugs. Live with the loss. Take out a loan on the house. Maybe one on the shipping business and the barge as well. They were free and clear. The bank would have no hesitation. He could pay off both once the casinos were up and running.

But did he want to step that close to the edge? Put everything on the line? What if the casinos went bust? He'd be in hock for years.

Either way time was working against him. He'd have to move fast.

He looked around the room. So full of memories, as he'd recently pointed out to Joe. His eyes fell on the collection of valuable calabashes.

He immediately averted them but it was too late. An idea had seated itself in his mind.

Keys rattled outside the front door.

"It's open," he shouted.

Helen came in carrying two full shopping bags.

"My feet are killing me," she said, kicking off her shoes. "How was your meeting at the hotel this morning?"

"Went well. Few things to work out but we're on the way. Looks like you had a successful shopping trip. All that for your trip?"

"Yes, I only hope I haven't forgotten anyone. Noses are so quick to go out of joint. I'm also going to visit Ni'ihau. Been ages since I was last there."

"Better brush up on your Hawaiian."

Helen laughed.

"Don't be silly, Albert. Hawaiian is my first language. That stays with you all of your life."

Only Hawaiian is spoken on the small island of Ni'ihau situated off Kauai.

"Joe should go there with you sometime." Albert said.

"Why would he want to do that? He hardly ever comes here anymore, much less trekking over to there."

"Be good for him to find out a little more about who he is. I'm talking about traditions. Blood ties. I haven't told you this, Helen, but I'm thinking of having Joe come here and work with me."

"My goodness, have you approached him about that?"

"I brought it up when he was here for the funeral."

"What did he say?"

"He didn't get get a chance to say anything. Lillian interrupted us in the middle of our talk."

"Honestly, do you really believe Joe would quit his job and go to work for you? I can't imagine Lillian would be happy about having to leave Honolulu, either."

Albert smiled.

"I was just talking with a man who has his eye on the future and is doing something about it now. We're going into business together. This is going to be big, Helen. All over the islands. And there is a place in it for Joe. He'll have no trouble seeing that he'd have a better future coming on board with me than staying with the police department once he hears what's involved. He won't walk away from that. And I believe Lillian will agree to come as well."

~~~

"Look at him," Walt Douglas said, pointing at the TV monitor. "He was trying to be so cool but see how he started to shift around? We had him dead to rights and he knew it. The game was over. He would've confessed in another minute. I'd put money on it."

The three detectives were watching the video playback of the Olomano interview. They'd returned to the room after everyone had left the police station .

"Not sure if his conscience was bothering him, though," Lam said. "He could've been just trying to figure out his next move. Lucky for him the lawyer showed up."

"Sure saved his butt," Walt said regretfully.

"You know, it's ironic that their lawyer used to be the Assistant City Attorney and his replacement has filed a misdemeanor charge on Kedron," Joe said.

The playback showed Sterling Huddleson entering the interview room, the officer standing outside looking embarrassed. Lam stopped the tape.

"Is that supposed to be some kind of weird karma we're up against?" Walt joked.

"No, just lucky for Olomano that Huddleson came when he did," Joe said "Like he was lucky getting that last Coke, too. Guy's charmed, I'm telling you."

Walt laughed.

"Maybe that luck will have run out the next time we see him," he said. "And to think he had the balls to demand his car back on his way out the door."

"Well, that's not going to happen anytime soon," Lam said firmly. "Although I wouldn't be surprised if we start getting flak from the lawyer."

"Run that tape back to where Walt mentioned our phantom witness," Joe said. "I'd like to take another look."

Lam replayed the scene. Joe concentrated on Kedron.

"Yeah, Walt really hit a nerve about having a witness," he said. "I think we should consider there might really be someone who saw the whole thing. I know that one person you talked with mentioned he'd heard what sounded like a drag race. Also said a lot of street racing goes on around there. You'd come looking for that kind of action if you owned a car like Olomano's, I'd imagine."

"It's a long shot but it's the best thing we have at the moment anyway," Lam agreed. "I'll check with traffic about that. Could be some hotrod owners they know we could talk with. Doubt if any of them would rat out one of their buddies but there's always a chance."

"The newspaper could run a followup story, too," Joe suggested. "Maybe a feature on illegal street racing."

"No one has come forward since the initial accident story," Lam said. "I'll call the paper and bring them up to date on the investigation. Maybe they'll run a followup story. Give a telephone number any witness can use. Guarantee anonymity."

"We done here?" Walt asked.

"Guess so," Lam told him. "Good work, gentlemen. Thanks."

"I should stop by the office and show my face," Walt told Joe. "I'll drop you off at Lillian's on the way."

Chapter 21

"Joe knew the victim, lieutenant," Walt Douglas said. "He was a street snitch Joe used when he worked patrol. Smalltime thief. Never anything violent. Joe thought it was unusual that the guy was carrying drugs, obviously with the intent to sell, when he was killed. Said he'd never been involved in dealing."

Douglas was in Lieutenant Ito's office. He'd been summoned there the moment he'd walked into the detectives' room.

"That doesn't give Detective Cheo the authority to work on another department's case," Ito told him. "He has his own assignments here. Who is this Detective Lam?"

"Detective Curtis Lam is the lead on the hit-and-run," Walt said. "Joe was just following up on the damaged car he'd seen in Waimea. Thought it would be helpful. In the spirit of inter-department cooperation. that is."

"You're pouring gas on the fire, detective. He had no business going to Waimea either. There again, meddling in another department. I specifically ordered him to stay out of that. How long have you been involved in this thing with him?"

Douglas shrugged.

"Not all that long. Bouncing off ideas between us mainly."

"Well, those ideas are being bounced on this department's time and using its resources. I have to account for them. Where is Detective Cheo, by the way?"

"Home with his wife, I guess. He's on compassionate leave taking care of her. I understand she's doing better."

Douglas wisely decided not to mention that he'd just dropped off Joe on their way back from the other police station. Nor that they'd conducted an interview with a person of interest in the hit-and-run investigation.

Ito raised his eyebrows.

"Thank you for the update on his wife," he said sarcastically. "I'm aware of Detective Cheo being on temporary leave. More pertinent at the moment, however, is the head of detectives at that other station you both have taken up with called to thank our captain for the help. I didn't know what the hell the captain was talking about when he told me. Came as a total surprise. Three detectives from two departments working on a single hit- and-run? This isn't a crime wave we're fighting, detective. I don't know how that other department is handled but I try to run a tight ship here. Do you see how that makes me look?"

Captain Queeg from the Caine Mutiny crossed Douglas's mind. He was glad Joe wasn't here. He would take the fall himself, if there was to be one.

"Anyway, it appears that they're making some progress over there on the investigation," Ito said. "So here's what's happening here in the meantime. Your case load in this department comes first. You keep an accurate record of your time spent working it. And I'll expect quick results. The same will go for Detective Cheo when he returns to duty. And if there is a solve on that hit-and-run, then the other department shares it with us. I want you to personally make sure of that."

Never one to miss an opportunity for glory, Douglas thought.

"I'll stay on top of it, lieutenant," he said.

~~~

Lillian had been out when Joe arrived at the apartment and had now just come in.

"You're home early," she said. "How was work?"

"Kind of fun," he said. "Felt good, actually. Surprised you weren't here, though. What's up?"

"I was also having fun doing the same thing," she teased. "Working. And, yes, it also felt good to me."

"Doctor okay with that? Your leaving here?"

"What he doesn't know won't hurt him."

Joe frowned.

"I'm thinking more of what could hurt you," he said. "Shouldn't you have called him first? I mean, a concussion isn't anything to play around with."

"I'm fine, Joe. Please don't worry. I just went to check on a couple of sources for that Maui job. I'm already behind schedule. Next thing, they'll be hiring someone else."

"They'd be crazy if they did," Joe said. "You're the best."

"Best is a fickle word in my business. The thing is, I really do need to get out of the house and back to work before I go completely nuts. Which brings up another subject. Our present living arrangement."

"What about about it?"

"Well, frankly, I guess we should talk about returning to the way it was."

"I'm all right with staying here a while longer."

"I could be all right with that, too. But I'm trying to be practical. I've loved your being here and taking care of me. It was sweet. However, I'm back on my feet now. Raring to go. Ready, willing and able. Need I say more?"

"I think I got it."

"Good. We were fortunate enough to discover something special about ourselves. We're a loving couple that needs a certain space. No one understands. You don't. I don't. All we know is that it works for us. Things couldn't be better in our marriage as long as we stick to that. Call it our unique marital dichotomy, for lack of a better explanation. I don't want to risk taking a chance on anything that might change it."

Joe smiled at her.

"How about I just spend tonight here? Head home in the morning."

Lillian returned the smile.

"I love you, Joe Cheo," she said. "Incidentally, did you ever tell Helen and Albert about my accident?"

Joe thought for a moment.

"Now that you mention it, I don't believe I did," he said, somewhat surprised at himself. "Guess there was so much going on that I didn't even think of it."

"Doesn't matter," Lillian said.

Though she would've been curious about how they might have reacted, especially Helen.

Chapter 22

Joe had left Lillian's before sunup to drive back to his apartment. It'd felt a little strange to be returning. He had gotten used to being around her all the time. More notably, he'd enjoyed it.

The place was a little musty and he opened the balcony door to let in some fresh air. He stepped out onto it to see the brightening eastern sky. The city hadn't fully awakened but he could hear that the surf at Waikiki was up. He turned to go back in and noticed his dad's old surfboard standing against the wall. He was still officially on leave. Why not?

⁓⁓⁓⁓

Gentle waves rolled toward the beach, evenly spaced in perfect sets of threes before breaking into bright foaming white caps. The occasional silver flash of a fish in their clear walls of water. A slight off-shore breeze made for perfect surfing conditions.

Most of the thirty thousand or so people who hit the beach on any day of the week were still in bed, so Joe had arrived at the best time.

He walked across the cool sand with the long board under his arm, its ankle strap on his right foot. He was a goofy and rode with his left foot forward. Holding the board in front of him, he launched into the water and began to paddle out.

The beach now distant, he sat up on the board and felt the ocean's pulse against his legs. He sensed the sea's breathing as he rose and fell with the swell, his own breathing seemingly in synchrony.

He was a speck on a living blue host.

His eyes wandered to Pearl Harbor and where the Arizona lay. He pictured the ship resting on the bottom, fish swimming along the dark companionways and compartments inside the broken hull. Some of those fish could be passing under him at this very moment. Even the water buoying his board might have flowed with the currents throughout her. Beyond belief.

He thought of the men entombed below her decks. They belonged to this beautiful island and are each and every one a part of its heritage.

The swell lifts him high and he points his board down the trough, picking up speed along the face of the developing wave now sweeping toward the beach. In the breaking crest, he sees a line of long boards joining up, their riders dressed in Class A uniforms of starch-white foam, the wrecked Arizona's full complement of men. They roar along with him and then disappear in tattered spindrift.

He feels the warm wind on his body as he shifts his weight in harmony with the board's motion rushing toward Oahu, the gathering place of kings.

The wave spent, he kicks off the board in shallow water. Rather than paddle out for another ride, he walks to the beach.

A beach boy was setting up his rental stand for the day. Umbrellas, swim fins, suntan lotion, a few surfboards, whatever and every thing.

"Looking good out there, bro," he called to Joe.

"Thanks," Joe said, stopping for a moment to chat. "Been awhile. Need some practice."

"Like riding a bicycle, bro. You never forget. Great board you got."

"Yeah, belonged to my dad. Goes way back."

"Thought it was an early one. Long board's the best. Easy to paddle, easy to ride. Can't beat that combination. You wouldn't consider selling that old board, would you? I'll make you a good offer."

Joe glanced back at the ocean before answering.

"You know, if you'd asked me yesterday, I would've said yes."

Chapter 23

"Late as usual, detective," Lola Kahamena scolded playfully. "Must mean things are back to normal."

Joe had just walked into the detectives' room.

"How is your wife?" she asked.

"Fine. She kicked me out this morning. The lieutenant in?"

"Smart lady," Lola said and pointed towards his office.

The door was open. Ito was busying himself with a pile of papers on his desktop. He looked up when Joe knocked.

"My wife has improved enough to be on her own, lieutenant," Joe said. "You can return me to the active duty roster."

"Ours or theirs?"

"Sir?"

"Detective Douglas will explain everything. Be sure you understand."

Ito waved him off and returned to the papers.

Joe had no idea what was meant by that but thought it better not to ask. Instead he thanked him and left.

"You come in to clean out your desk?" Walt Douglas wisecracked.

"Maybe I should ask you the same thing," Joe said, sitting down. "No, I'm officially back on the job. Lillian's well enough so she doesn't need me there. Ito said you'd fill me in about something."

"Let's go up to the roof," Walt said.

In sight of the Arizona Memorial, Walt recounted his conversation with the lieutenant.

"He had a hemorrhage about the time sheets," Walt said. "We have to write down every damn minute."

"He's always having a hemorrhage over time sheets," Joe said. "He's a career pencil pusher. That's all he knows. Nice of that other station to call, though."

"The good thing is Ito didn't pull us off the hit-and-run," Walt said. "He smells a case solve he can take credit for. He's starving for one."

"Well, let's hope he gets it. Make everybody happy."

"'Speaking of happy, today is Bee's birthday. How about you and Lillian coming over tonight to help us celebrate it?"

"She's playing catch-up on a big job in Maui," Joe said. "Fell way behind when she was home recovering. I'll call her but I doubt if she'll want to break away from it."

~~~

Albert had gotten a troubling surprise. Helen's name was also listed on the titles to both the house and tugboat barge business. A codicil had been added. He'd just removed the documents from the safe in the main house in preparation to looking into taking out a loan on the properties.

Obviously, George had done this without telling him. But why? Being the eldest son, George had been given the house and business by their father. That was a tradition the head of the family had always followed upon the eldest son's having reached a certain age. In this case, Albert would naturally be next in line. For some reason, George had broken with that. And worse, he had died leaving everything to Helen as the lone survivor.

Did she even realize that?

Well, he certainly realizes where this leaves him.

~~~

Walt lived in a condominium a little beyond the Punchbowl. It was a two-story wooden structure on a quiet street. His was an end unit with a lanai that wrapped around the corner, giving a view of the green mountains. Banana trees and red-flowered ginger plants landscaped the grounds.

Joe parked out front. He'd bought a bottle of champagne that Lillian had recommended. He'd been right about her feeling unable to spare the time, though she was genuinely disappointed.

He rang the door bell and a man opened it.

"Happy Birthday, Bee!" Joe said.

Bee was a nickname. His given name was Bruce Ferebee. He and Walt were partners and had been together for ten years.

"Thanks, Joe. Where's Lillian?"

"She couldn't come. She's behind on a new job and is trying to get back up to speed. Said to give you her love and to please forgive her."

"Sorry she couldn't make it but I can understand. Walt's in the kitchen. Please, come in."

"Lillian sent you this," Joe said, handing him the champagne.

A note tied around the bottle's neck read: 'Happy Birthday to a now even older friend'.

"Funny girl," he said, checking the label. "Wow, she knows her stuff."

Apparently so, Joe thought, considering what it'd cost him.

Walt, sporting a blue apron, was chopping some spinach on a cutting board when they came into the kitchen.

"Lillian blew her life's savings on this," Bee said, holding up the bottle for him to see. "Better put it on ice for later."

"Get Joe a drink while you're at it, Bee. I'm going to be here for awhile getting this thing organized."

"He ran across an obscure recipe for a vegetable casserole," Bee explained. "He's been on a health kick lately. The recipe itself isn't all that complicated, just takes forever. Red wine okay?"

"Sure," Joe said. "Forgot you were so into cooking, Walt."

"Both of us are serious about it. In fact, that's how we met. We were taking a Cordon Bleu course. This just happens to be my week at the stove. Bee takes command next week."

"You bake that cake over there on the table, Walt?" Joe asked. "Looks good."

"I baked it." Bee corrected, pouring Joe a glass of wine and also topping off his and Walt's. "He flunked baking."

"Teacher's fault," Walt joked.

"Actually, I had yesterday afternoon off and thought it'd be fun to bake myself a cake," Bee explained.

"Here's to the birthday boy," Walt said, raising his glass.

No one in the department knew that Walt was gay. He preferred it remained that way, too. Bruce's nickname helped. Most thought Bee was a woman. Walt avoided any department functions that might include a family. Homosexuality was no longer a crime and a lot of progress had been made since the NYC police raided the Stonewall Inn but attitudes are slow to change. Especially among cops.

Joe had proved to be an exception.

Walt had taken a chance on confiding in him when he and Bee were going through a rough patch. It had come to the point where it was affecting his job. He was distracted and that could put both Joe and himself in danger.

Seeing a marriage counselor wasn't an option. Joe was the only person he felt he could trust.

Joe had sympathized with his situation. He told him that his and Lillian's relationship had once become rocky without either of them realizing. They had agreed on a trial separation, which led them to a remarkable discovery that not only saved their marriage but made it even better. He wasn't saying that what they did would work for others. What that might be, only they could find out. Just keep an open mind and let the chips fall.

Not too long afterward Walt and Bee were able to smooth things out.

They'd since regarded Joe and Lillian as special friends.

"Why don't you two go out on the lanai?" Walt suggested. "I can work here better alone."

The table there had been set for four people. Bee grabbed up the unneeded setting and took it back inside.

Joe thought about Walt and how tough it must be to have to lead a double life. One here, one there. Nothing ever settled. Just back and forth in a masquerade. Sounded like himself in a way. Always between islands.

He looked at the mountains. The sun was getting low and the green foliage had darkened. A stillness began to fall as birds winged to their roosts and silenced themselves. It would soon be night and a new order would take over.

"You have a million dollar view out here," Joe said when Bee returned.

"Soon will be at the way prices are rising," Bee said.

"Reminds me of Viet Nam," Joe said quietly. "The terrain and all."

"I never made it there. Missed the draft."

"Be glad."

The mention of the war and the fading light unleashed a flashback in Joe's mind. He was in a jungle clearing. Normally, he would've just shrugged it off. But this one was staying put. He began to feel anxious.

"Always wondered how it was in Viet Nam," Bee said. "You hear all kinds of stuff. Don't know how much of it is true. Sometimes I wished I'd gone."

Joe wished he would shut up. He wasn't doing well with this. He couldn't hold it back any longer. He had to talk.

"I'll give you an example of how it was," he said. "Ever hear of a puzzle about three guards in a room with two doors? One guard lies, one sometimes lies and one always tells the truth. One door leads to freedom. The other door doesn't. You ask each guard which door to take. How do you know who's being truthful?"

Bee laughed.

"What's that have to do with Viet Nam? Anyway, that's an old high school math problem. You solve it with permutations."

"I once saw an ARVN officer solve it with a Colt 45 automatic," Joe said. "That's a sidearm, in case you didn't know.

Bee gave him a quizzical look.

"There were three Viet Cong we'd captured after a firefight. My unit had joined up with the ARVNs for the battle. It was pretty bloody. They were the only VC survivors and we stood them together in a clearing. It was getting dark kind of like it is here now. Our intelligence suspected the VC in that area had important information that they needed to know. A lot of lives could be at stake. The ARVN officer asked them each a single question."

Bee squinted, as if trying to see where this was going.

"What was the question?" he asked.

"The location of a NVA battalion moving down the Ho Chi Minh trail."

"Which one told the truth?"

"The last one standing."

The memory mercifully subsided for Joe. An awkward silence followed between the two men.

"I better go see how Walt's doing," Bee said. "Excuse me."

The casserole had been completed in short order once Walt had gotten going. Everyone agreed it was worth the wait. The earlier conversation about Viet Nam was forgotten.

"That champagne chilled enough?" Walt asked, as they were finishing the last of their meal. "We can have it with the cake."

"The French would riot in the street if you did that," Bee said. 'We'll have the cake with coffee."

"He overstates everything," Walt said to Joe.

Bee carefully removed the cork without it making even a hiss.

"Never pop the cork," he said. "It disturbs the balance. Just work it out nice and easy."

They toasted each other and sang Happy Birthday for Bee.

"Picked up a new client," Bee said later, over coffee and cake. "Though I doubt if they'll be ordering this champagne."

Bee managed a beverage distribution company that mainly serviced hotels. It'd recently expanded the service to include a bar.

"Clientele there is beer and cheap wine," he added.

"My kind of place," Joe said. "What's its name?"

"The Asterisk," Bee told him. "Over in Pearl."

Joe suddenly remembered the key with the asterisk imprint and number he'd found in Ricky Ricola's apartment. Could it belong to a locker? Lot of military stationed around Pearl. They sometimes rent lockers, especially when they're shipping out for a tour. But why would Ricky have rented one? He's as far away from being in the military as you can get. And hidden the key in the toilet? Could all be coincidental except he never put much faith in coincidences.

"Where is it in Pearl?" he asked.

"I'll have to get the address from the office. Don't tell me you're planning to hang out there."

Chapter 24

Madalyn Crocker's bedside alarm clock rang precisely at 6:21 a.m. She reached over and hit the snooze button. That gave her an extra nine minutes to luxuriate in bed and let any earlier thoughts that might've keep her awake half the night have their say now. It was a trick she'd practiced for years.

Her love life came to mind. At present, it was nonexistent.

It wasn't that she was panting or anything for the lack there of. She just didn't know anyone outside of work. And she had always made it a rule to stay clear of the workplace.

And besides, who would it be there anyway?

Harlan Faison seemed to be a nice enough guy but nothing clicked. Also, he was her boss. Strictly off limits.

Sterling Huddleston had attempted a run at her when she had first come to town. She hadn't known he was married then. Uh-uh.

That police detective who'd written the reports was cute. What's his name? Oh, yeah, Joe Cheo. Smart, too. He would qualify as being outside of work. But he was married and had principles. She wasn't a home wrecker.

There was the esoteric side of her eroticism to consider as well.

Maybe she should try to take in more social events. Meet new people. Boring but you never know.

Then there was the person she had seen at the Olomano party who seemed familiar. Nothing to do with her love life but she now remembered his name. John Sutton. Her late husband knew him.

The snooze alarm went off. 6:30 a.m. on the dot.

She was at her desk an hour and a half later. She picked up her phone and dialed her old boss in the Las Vegas city attorney's office.

~~~

Joe Cheo had lain awake half the night thinking about the Asterisk. He should've been dead tired when his alarm rang but remarkably he'd felt good. Excited even.

He'd jumped out of bed, gotten dressed and left early for work.

"This thing must be broken," Lola Kahamena said, examining her watch, when he came into the detectives' room.

"Turning over a new leaf," Joe said, signing in and then heading straight for his desk.

Walt wasn't in yet. He wondered if the birthday party had continued without him. He gave a little smile at that and dialed the Asterisk's number. He'd looked it up last night but decided to wait until now to call.

"Asterisk," a man answered. "We don't open until ten."

"I'm interested in a locker rental," Joe said. "Your ad in the Yellow Pages said you have them."

"They're twenty bucks a month rent. Twenty bucks deposit for the key. You military?"

"Ex-Army. How big are the lockers?"

"Like those you had in high school. Where'd you serve?"

"Viet Nam."

"Then make it fifteen bucks a month. Forget the key deposit."

"You going to be there for awhile?"

"Yeah, I'm the owner."

He thanked the man and hung up.

He unlocked his desk drawer and removed a small manila envelope. The key was inside still protected by the glassine evidence envelope he'd originally put it in.

Should he wait for Walt to arrive? What about bringing Curtis Lam into the picture? Aren't we all supposed to be working together? What did he expect to find in the locker? That is, assuming this key even belongs to a locker at the Asterisk.

He stuck the envelope back in the drawer and locked it.

"When Detective Douglas comes in, tell him I'm on the roof," he told Lola.

He stopped by the tiny kitchen and saw that a pot of coffee had been freshly made. He silently thanked whoever was responsible and poured a cup to take with him.

No one else was on the roof. Not that he expected there would be. He walked over to the edge and stood, sipping his coffee. Someone should put a couple of chairs out here, he thought. Maybe a beach umbrella would be nice, too.

Clouds were beginning to gather on the hills beyond the harbor with the promise of a possible shower. A possible omen? Or they could just blow away.

He realizes that he should've mentioned the key to Walt. There was no need for him not to have. As it has now turned out, it could be very important to the case.

He could say it simply slipped his mind. What with everything else going on that's not only reasonable but entirely possible. In fact, he hadn't thought about the damn thing until Bee mentioned the Asterisk.

He'll just have to follow the advice he'd given Walt back when he and Bee were having a problem. Let the chips fall. Pick 'em up one at a time.

"Lola said you were up here," Walt called from the doorway.

~~~

Walt had just shaken his head in exasperation when Joe told him about the key and mumbled something about being in for a penny. Then he had gone back to his desk without saying another word.

After things had calmed a little between them, Joe called Curtis Lam and they agreed to meet at the Asterisk. Lam got there first and had parked a few doors past the bar and was waiting in his car when Walt and Joe pulled in behind him.

The Asterisk was now open. The bartender was sitting on a stool at the end of the bar reading the newspaper when the three detectives came in. No one else was there.

"Good morning," he said getting up and stepping behind the bar. "What can I get for you?"

"Are you the person I spoke with on the phone this morning about the lockers?" Joe asked.

"No, that must've been Danny. He's the owner. Stepped out for a minute. You want to rent one? I can help you with that."

He reached beneath the bar and pulled out a ledger.

"Just need some information actually," Joe smiled. "What's your name?"

"Keanu. Have you been here before? Can't place you."

"First time I've been here, Keanu, My name is Detective Joe Cheo and I'm with the Honolulu Police Department."

Joe showed him his badge.

"These two gentlemen with me are Detectives Walt Douglas and Curtis Lam. I'd like you to look at a key and tell me if it belongs to one of your lockers."

He removed the key from the evidence envelope in his briefcase and held it up for the bartender to see.

"This key belong to any of your lockers?" he asked.

"Could be one of ours," Keanu said cautiously, taking a closer look. "Yep, number two-eight-zero. Somebody turn it in or what? Seems kind of funny the police coming here to give it back."

"I'll get to that in a minute," Joe said. "Does that ledger you're holding list the names of the rentals? I'd like to know who rented this one."

"Uh, I'm not sure if I should tell you. We respect our renters privacy. Don't you need a warrant for this kind of thing?"

"We can get a warrant," Walt jumped in. "Also, we might like to open the locker this key fits. We'll get one for that as well. Have to shut you down while we wait for them to be processed."

A man came into the bar.

"Is there a problem, gentlemen?" he asked, walking up to the group.

"They're cops, Danny," Keanu told him. "Here about the lockers."

"I'm Dan Ellis. I own this place. What can I do for you?"

"Mr. Ellis," Joe said. "I'm Detective Joe Cheo. We spoke earlier this morning."

"You the guy who called me about renting a locker?" Ellis asked suspiciously. "Said you were a vet. Was that some kind of bullshit?"

"I am a veteran, sir. And as I just said, I'm also a detective. We have a key that may be evidence in a criminal investigation. Your bartender identified it as belonging to one of your lockers. We need the name of the person who rented that locker and we need to open it."

"I told them they had to have a warrant, Danny," Keanu said.

"If that's necessary, we can get one," Joe said.

"Then go get a damn warrant," Ellis said smartly. "I don't need this crap."

"As you wish, Mr. Ellis," Joe said. "We'll make a request for a warrant. It may take a couple of days before the judge can sign it, so your bar will have to remain closed until then."

Ellis glared at him.

"Or we could just cut to the chase," Joe said with a friendly smile. "Save everybody a lot of time and bother. We'll get the name whichever you decide. Your call."

151

"What was the locker number?" Ellis grumbled, grabbing the ledger from Keanu.

"Two-eight-zero," Joe answered.

Ellis ran his finger down the page and turned to the next.

"Here it is," he said. "Richard Ricola. Actually, he rented a couple of lockers. That one you've got and two-seven-zero. You wrote them up, Keanu."

"Do you require any ID for your rentals?" Joe asked.

"Drivers license or military ID card," Keanu replied.

"Ricola's drivers license was invalid," Joe said.

"Didn't notice," Keanu said. "I just put down the military ID number or the drivers license number."

"Here's a copy of his license," Joe said. "Numbers match?"

"Yeah, that's him," Keanu said. "He rented both lockers. Two-eight-zero and two-seven-zero."

"Wait a minute, two-seven-zero was the locker that jerk came in raising all kinds of hell about something missing out of it," Ellis said. "Wanted me to open all the lockers. Told him to forget it. He got ugly. I called the cops but he left before they came. Asshole was so pissed off he forgot to lock his own locker. I shut it and put the key back on the board."

"Did he give his name?" Joe asked.

"No, I assumed he'd rented it. Didn't check the ledger."

"You remember what he looked like?"

"Scary bastard. Mean eyes. Not as tall as you."

"Has he been back since then?" Walt asked.

"No, but I've got something waiting for him the next time," Ellis said, nodding toward a baseball bat stationed under the bar.

"That Ricola guy was here the night after he rented the lockers," Keanu said. "Sat at the bar nursing a beer for a damn hour and we were busier than hell. Then he showed up again the other day. Maybe he took whatever that guy was all shook up about."

"Ricky Ricola was here again?" Joe asked. "Let's take a look at two-eight-zero. What was the other locker, two-seven-zero?"

"Yeah, it's right beside it."

The room contained forty lockers in two rows with one stacked on the other. They were all painted an institutional green and surprisingly looked new.

"Lockers came from a private school that decided they didn't need them," Ellis said. "Had them in storage. Brand new. Never been used."

"I can see that," Joe said.

"Try to keep 'em looking good, too," Ellis told him. "Wipe down each locker inside and out before it's rented again. Here's two-eight-zero."

Joe slipped on a pair of gloves and carefully removed the key from the envelope. He put it in the lock and opened the door. There was an empty shelf in the top half. A medium size overnight bag sat in the bottom. He bent down and carefully zipped it open.

Douglas and Lam peered over his shoulder.

Joe muttered something and zipped shut the bag.

"Mr. Ellis, I'm sorry but now you really do have to close the bar," he said. "We'll do the best we can to get you back open. Hopefully, it'll just take a couple of hours."

He turned to Douglas and Lam.

"Curtis, your narcotics team need to come here," he said. "We should have a forensics examination done on both lockers, too."

"What the hell was in that bag?" Lam asked.

"I think this is where Ricky Ricola got his codpiece."

Chapter 25

"John Sutton is the go-to person when you need something done in Las Vegas." Madalyn Crocker said. "Openly or on the quiet."

She was in Harlan Faison's office.

"He knows people in high places. He's tight with the gaming commission. The casino owners. Politicians. Certain other elements in town who prefer to remain anonymous. He occasionally works both sides of the fence."

"And this Sutton is the same person you thought you recognized at the party?" Faison asked.

"Yes, I couldn't place him then. Maybe he's had some work done on his face. Eyes tightened or whatever. Plastic surgery is another Las Vegas industry. But his name came to me this morning. That's why I called my old boss. To see if they knew of anything going on that Sutton might be involved with. Could be something coming up that someone else wants to keep under his hat until it's ready for prime time."

"How did you get to know Sutton?"

"My late husband knew him. The two of them would drop by the casino where I worked. In fact, that's where I met my husband. Eugene owned an import business in Los Angeles. He was expanding his operation to include Las Vegas. He was commuting between LA and Vegas when he died in a car accident. I really never knew all that much about his business, so I can't say for certain that there was anything between them on that account. But I wouldn't be surprised if there had been."

"Did you find out anything from the Las Vegas city attorney?"

"Nothing specific. Or at least nothing they're willing to talk about. But those certain other elements in town that I mentioned? They rarely bet on even odds. They like a sure thing."

"I see, so what's your take on Sutton's being at the party?"

"Las Vegas wants in on the gambling. He's working on improving the odds of the bill's passing."

~~~

Albert was beside himself. His patience had about run out. He was at the point of becoming furious. Why was she behaving this way?

He and Helen were in the living room of the main house. Helen sat in an easy chair. Albert paced back and forth.

"Helen, you are being impossible," he scolded from near the front window. "How many times do I have to tell you there's nothing to worry about? Be reasonable for once and listen to me."

"Agreeing to mortgage everything we have is being reasonable?" Helen asked. "We don't owe a dime to anyone. Why start now?"

"Businesses do that all the time," Albert said, stopping in front of her. "They put up collateral to borrow money for financing new investments. That's how they grow. You have to plan for the future."

"And what happens if they're wrong?" Helen asked, cocking her head slightly.

"Important people are involved in this project, Helen. They don't make mistakes."

"Who are these people?"

"They prefer to remain unknown while the negotiations are going on," Albert said, brushing off the question. "You wouldn't recognize their names anyway. Please, all you have to do is sign the papers. You don't have to go to the lawyer's office. He'll come here. I'll handle everything after that."

"I wonder what George would've done," she said wistfully. "Would he have been reasonable?"

"He would have signed the damn papers," Albert snapped. "Like he would want you to do now."

"Maybe, maybe not. But it's no longer his decision, is it? It's mine. And I want to think about it a while longer. Those important people of yours will just have to wait."

Albert rubbed at his eyes. He suddenly felt very tired.

"Helen, an opportunity like this doesn't come along very often," he said quietly. "We stand to make a lot of money. It'd be foolish to pass it up."

"Albert, we don't need a lot money. I'm very happy with the way things are at the present. And frankly, I intend to keep them that way."

"What about Joe? This is for him, too."

"I think Joe can take care of himself."

~~~

"Four bags with a kilo in each were in the locker, lieutenant," Joe said. "One had been cut open. Whoever bought the stuff probably tested it first. Ricola more than likely got the drugs he had on him from that bag. Detective Lam's narcotics squad believes they'll match the other. Might be able to tell where it was produced. Could provide a lead. Maybe not much, but something. One thing they did discover was the heroin had been cut a few times. Kind of unusual for an initial buy of that quantity. You'd expect it would be pure. Wonder if whoever bought it paid top dollar thinking it was. Be a joke on him."

He and Walt had just returned from the Asterisk and were in Ito's office giving him a rundown on what they'd found at the bar. The lieutenant was seated behind his desk. The two detectives sat in chairs to the side. It was late afternoon and the shifts were about to change.

"Lam also brought in a forensics team to dust the lockers," Walt said. "Got a few prints. Don't know how good. They'll do the same with the bags. Hopefully, we can identify them. Of course, that might take some time. They're pretty slow."

Ito nodded without commenting. That had been his reaction to everything they'd reported so far. Walt exchanged a quick glance with Joe.

"Yeah, that's always the case," Joe said. "There's a new ID system that speeds things up. Called AFIS. Stands for automated fingerprint identification system. Lot of departments on the mainland have it now. FBI, too. Actually, the system's been out for a few years. Maybe we'll have it here some day. Right, lieutenant?"

No comment.

"Back to the lockers," Joe continued. "Ricky Ricola rented both of them. Name's on the rental ledger. Also, the bartender remembered him. But I believe they were rented for someone else. We do know that another person had a key to one locker. Bar's owner said he complained about something being taken from it. Raised hell, in fact. That locker was empty when we opened it. Inexplicably, Ricky had the key to the locker full of drugs. I just can't see him putting them there. Possibly it was the second person he'd rented it for. My money is on Frank Lofume being that person. But what was Ricky doing with the key? And both of them now dead. Lofume a homicide, Ricola a fatal accident afterwards. And the mysterious other person with the empty locker. I think somehow all of this is tied together but I can't see the string."

"That key turned up in Ricola's apartment when it was gone through after he was killed in the hit-and-run, lieutenant," Walt added.

He purposely didn't say who had gone through the apartment. Nor who'd turned up the key.

"Detective Lam's having the newspaper run another article on that accident, asking for witnesses," Joe said.

"Long shot," Walt said. "The first story was all about the drugs they found on Ricola. Made him look like a big time dealer. People will be afraid to say anything. Still worth the effort, though."

"Maybe they'll play down the drug angle this time," Joe said. "Anyway, that's where we are at the present, lieutenant."

Ito nodded.

"Be sure to include the hours you spent working with the other department on your timesheets," he said. "Now if you'll excuse me, I have to be somewhere."

Joe and Walt thanked him and went back to their desks.

"What do you make of that?" Walt asked.

"I can't," Joe said. "Something has to be going on."

"You seeing Lillian tonight?"

"No, I'm home. She's still working."

"Want to have a drink somewhere?"

"There's a bar not too far from here. Used to be on my beat. Better fill out our timesheets first, though."

~~~

The bar at Papa Din's was standing room only. All the tables were taken, save for a couple of small ones which had reserved signs on them. Like its namesake, a steady din of conversation and laughter roiled throughout the room.

"Looks like happy hour has gone into overtime," Joe said, waiting at the entrance. "You want to try some place else?"

"Little space at the end of the bar," Walt said. "Let's go for it."

They made their way down.

"What are you having?" Joe asked.

"Scotch and soda," Walt said. "Make it light."

Joe edged up to the bar and ordered. He got a beer for himself.

"Better times," Walt toasted.

"And hopefully soon," Joe said, tipping his bottle.

They stood with the wall to their backs taking in the action.

"Was it always this popular?" Walt asked. "I mean when you were on the beat."

"Yep, just a different crowd," Joe said. "Not quite as uptown as it is now. Bee ought to check out the bar. Maybe he can get a piece."

"He's getting his feet wet first in the low-rent district."

"Well, he started in the right place with the Asterisk."

"That reminds me," Walt said. "When you told Ito that you believed Ricola rented the lockers for Lofume, this funny idea popped up in my mind. Was the gorilla who broke Lofume's neck in on the drugs with him? Is that crazy or what?"

Joe didn't comment. His attention was on a couple being seated at one of the reserved tables across the room.

"Don't look now but Lieutenant Ito and Assistant City Attorney Madalyn Crocker are joining us," he said, nodding toward them.

Walt turned to see.

"C'mon," Joe said. "There's a door in the kitchen."

They fell in behind a passing waiter and followed him.

"Hey, you two guys can't come in here," a cook yelled when they entered.

Joe flashed his badge.

"Where's the back door," he demanded.

The cook pointed to the rear.

"Thank you," Joe said. "Nothing to worry about, sir."

Half a minute later they were outside on the sidewalk.

"That was close," Walt said. "But now that I think of it, why'd we have to leave? Actually, I have a couple cases I want to file with her. Could've introduced myself. Would've been fun to have seen Ito's reaction, too."

"Just seemed like the smart thing to do at the moment," Joe said. "Do you want to go back in?"

"Not particularly. Do you suppose they're on a date?"

"I can't imagine that but who knows?"

"She's striking. I can understand now why he was so anxious to get rid of us."

"Well, it beats me how he did it but if he has something going with her then good for him."

"Might be good for everybody," Walt agreed. "Lighten him up a little."

"Before Ito showed up and interrupted, you were talking about the possibility of Frank Lofume knowing the person who killed him," Joe said.

"Yeah, it goes back to the lockers," Walt said. "Why did he need two? The drugs were only in one."

"Maybe he thought he might need them," Joe said.

"Four kilos wasn't exactly a small buy but it wasn't all that big space wise," Walt said. "He would've known how much room he'd need. One locker would have been large enough."

"All right, conjecture is as good as anything else at the moment. Where do you go from there?"

"Straight to the guy who had the empty locker. Let's say he was in on the drug deal with Lofume. But Lofume had other plans, like keeping the drugs for himself. So he switched the lockers. When the guy found out they were gone, he went bananas. I think he's the gorilla."

"But the timing's off. Frank was killed before that."

"Could be they wound up double-crossing each other and the gorilla got the short end of the stick with the drugs."

"How did Ricky wind up with the key?"

"He might've been in on the deal, too."

"I still can't see Ricky being involved in a drug deal. Not as a main player anyway. Way above his rank. I put him down as being a patsy."

"Well, maybe we'll eventually find out," Walt said. "There's one more thing we should concern ourselves with right now, Joe. As far as Lieutenant Ito knows, we're helping Lam with the hit-and-run. He seems to have signed off on that. Not sure how he would react to our being involved in a homicide with another department."

"Yeah, he'd have another hemorrhage for certain," Joe said. "It's just that we might be on to something."

"We might be on our way out of HPD if he finds out."

"What are you saying then, Walt? We should drop it?"

"No, I just think we'd better watch our step from here on. Work with Lam but let him take the credit. No more mentioning of our involvement to his lieutenant or anyone else."

"Should I make a note of that on my timesheet?"

Chapter 26

"I'll call a taxi," Helen said.

"Nonsense," Albert replied. "I can drive you to the airport. Give me a moment to finish up."

"I don't want to take you away from whatever it is you're doing."

Albert was busy inventorying everything in the house.

"It's nothing that can't wait until later, Helen."

The flight to Kauai wasn't due to leave General Lyman Field outside of Hilo for another two hours. Helen had packed the night before and had been dressed and ready to leave since early morning.

"You have the telephone number?" she asked.

"They still using the Hauoli Grocery Store's phone?"

"Yes."

"I have their number. Do you think the Robinsons will ever get electricity?"

"They're kama'aina, Albert. You should appreciate that."

Many Hawaiian old-timers possess a deep love of nature and strive to preserve the traditions of their culture. These values are often demonstrated through their lifestyles. To that end, the Robinsons had chosen to shun electricity.

Helen's closest friend was Alice Robinson. They'd both taught at the school in Hilo. After the tsunami nearly wiped it out, Alice moved back to her family home in Kauai. Helen loved to visit her there. The isolation was her refuge. The only contact with the outside world was through the telephone at the Hauoli Grocery Store.

"I don't want to be late for my flight, Albert. If you insist on driving me, we'd better go."

~~~

"Paper did a good job on that followup story," Walt Douglas said, handing the morning newspaper back to Joe. "Should get a lot of interest."

They were at their desks in the detectives' room.

"Too bad we couldn't give them a photo of Olomano's car to use," Joe said with a grin. "It'd be poetic."

"The department would get its pants sued off and we'd be hung out to dry," Walt laughed.

"Well, I do like the picture they did use," Joe said. "Car's kind of flashy like Olomano's. Might help to jar loose a memory for someone out there. Wonder whose car it is?"

"Probably belongs to the guy who wrote the article," Walt said. "Seemed to know a lot about drag strip racing. Not too keen on doing it on the public streets, however. Made a big point about that. Led with it right in to the request for information on the Ricola hit-and-run. Thought that was a nice touch. Lam is the contact for any calls that might bring. Could be a little late in the game, though."

"Not necessarily, Walt. If a person knows something and is holding back, that story is a reminder. His conscience could start bothering him. Might be a chance for him to get it off his chest."

"Suppose it could. We'll just have to wait and see. Not much more we can do. Same thing with the prints from those lockers. I should call Lam. Maybe he can light a fire under somebody at forensics."

"Don't hold your breath."

"The department ought to have that AFIS you mentioned, Joe. I can't figure out why we don't, can you?"

"Maybe it's too new. They're waiting to see."

"I'm going to run these reports over to Ito's girlfriend for filing, Joe. You want to tag along?"

"Better than sticking around here waiting for the phone to ring. Why don't we walk? It's not all that far and I could use the exercise."

Half-an-hour and a brisk walk later they were at the city hall. A clerk led them to the Assistant City Attorney's office and knocked on the side of the open door.

"Come in," Madalyn Crocker called out without looking up from her desk while continuing to read through some paperwork.

"Good morning, ma'am," Walt said. "I'm Detective Walt Douglas. I have some reports I'd like to have filed."

"Have a seat, detective," she said, still absorbed in the papers. "I'll be right with you."

"Good morning, ma'am," Joe said. "I'm Detective Joe Cheo."

She looked up.

"I'm with him," Joe said, pointing.

"Then you should also have a seat, Detective Cheo," she told him.

They both sat down.

"You mentioned having some reports that you'd like me to file, Detective Douglas?" she asked, putting the papers aside.

"Yes, they concern three burglary investigations I handled."

"You and Detective Cheo work together on them?"

"Not with these cases but off and on we do work together."

"I guess last night was an 'on', huh?"

"Ma'am?"

"I saw you both at Papa Din's."

"How did you…" Walt began.

"I checked out the room when I came in. Carryover from my working days and nights in the casino. Like to see who comes and goes. Recognized you two standing at the bar."

"Did the lieutenant..."

"Did he see you two? He never noticed a thing. But why did you both suddenly run out, Detective Douglas?"

"I remembered something I left at the office," Joe said, coming to the rescue. "Had to go back."

"Through the kitchen?"

"It was the quicker way out," Joe said.

"Must have been something important to have had to rush off like that. Too bad. You could have joined us. I would've liked that."

"We wouldn't have wanted to impose."

"Impose on what?"

Joe shifted on his feet and looked at Walt. He wished he had stayed back at the office.

"Oh, I get it now," Madalyn laughed, pausing to look from one to the other. "You saw us come in and thought the lieutenant and I were there on a date. Right?"

"It's none of our business, really," Walt said, embarrassed.

"This is so funny," Madalyn laughed again. "But please let me assure you that it was completely innocent. Nothing romantic at all. I knew your lieutenant's older sister in Las Vegas. She was a pit boss at the casino where I worked. One of the first women in the business to hold that job, by the way. We became friends and remain so today. When she learned that I was coming here, she told me that her brother was a lieutenant with the police department. She said they hadn't seen each other for some time and she'd been terrible about writing. So I thought he might like to know what she was up to. Papa Din's was convenient for me since I live just around the corner, that's all. A date, indeed. That's precious. And what would it have mattered to you anyway?"

Neither detective answered.

Then everyone broke up.

"Now, take me through those reports, Detective Douglas," Madalyn said after they'd all finished laughing.

Chapter 27

Albert had completed the inventory he'd started before driving Helen to the airport. She should have arrived in Kauai by now, he thought. Would the Robertsons meet her at the airport and drive her to their home? Maybe they've come to shunning automobiles as well.

As he read through the list he'd written, he realized that the calabash collection was the only item of real value they had. Even so, he doubted if that would bring any where near the amount of money he needed to raise. That said, would he even be able to sell them in time?

He balled up the piece of paper and tossed it on the floor. It was a stupid idea that showed how desperate he'd become. It was almost embarrassing.

If Helen had listened to him he wouldn't be in this position. He'd never known that she could be so stubborn. Was she like that with George? Someone knocked at the front door. He looked out the window and saw Tiny waiting there.

~~~

Ke-ke Greenlaw was scared. And angry. She didn't know which was worse. It was like they were both ganging up on her. At least she was no longer crying.

But now she just might've found a way to get back at that bastard boyfriend of hers for dumping her just like that!

But if she does what she's thinking, could she get in trouble, too? He's the one who was driving. There was nothing she could do really. Wasn't her fault. Anybody could see that. What if he finds out she told? That might not be a good thing for her. He wasn't a very nice person.

She decided to read the newspaper article again before making up her mind.

~~~

The morning had been relatively quiet for Detective Curtis Lam. He'd busied himself writing a few reports. Taken a couple of telephone calls of no real importance. He had hoped to have gotten some results from the newspaper article by now but so far nothing. Not even a prank call, which normally and sadly you'd expect. Lam's name and telephone number had been listed as the police contact. That was the usual practice on a smaller investigation. Something big would rate a generated number and be manned around the clock.

His phone rang.

"This is Detective Lam," he answered.

"I'm calling about the story on the accident that was in the paper today," a woman replied. "I have some information. The paper said I don't have to give you my name. Is that right?"

"That's true, ma'am. Certainly, it would be good to have it in case we needed to get back to you. And you would be completely anonymous as far as anyone else goes, but it you are more comfortable doing it this way that's fine with me. Please, go ahead."

"I saw the car that hit that poor man. It was racing."

"Racing another car or just speeding?" Lam asked, writing that down.

"Racing a pickup truck."

"This is really helpful, ma'am. Do you recall where you were at the time you saw the accident?"

The article hadn't included the location. Having that knowledge would further authenticate the caller and help to rule out any thrill-seekers.

"It was in Chinatown is all I remember."

He would have rather had something specific. He could come back to this.

"All right, can you describe the car that hit the man?"

"It was bright red with shiny fenders and the engine made a lot of noise. I think it was a Volkswagen but it didn't look like a regular one."

That was spot on.

"Did you happen to get its license plate number?"

"No."

That might've been too much to hope for.

"Okay, what about the truck?"

"It was a black Toyota."

"Was it customized like the red car?"

"It looked more regular but some."

"Did it also hit the pedestrian?"

"No, the red car was in front and it hit him. But the truck had a funny license. I remember it."

"That's fantastic."

"It was K-W-I-K-R. Stands for quicker."

Lam wrote that down and then hesitated before asking anything else. This conversation was starting to bother him. She knew a lot of details but couldn't remember where she had been other than in Chinatown. Could be due to the shock of witnessing the accident. However, she didn't sound like she was under stress nor very sympathetic to the victim. She didn't get the VW's plate but nailed the truck's right down to its meaning. This was definitely not a prank call but there was something going on with her other than just being a good citizen. He felt it was time to find out.

"Could you see who was driving the truck?" he asked.

"Just a guy."

"Well, he will possibly face a felony charge as being an accessory since the accident resulted in a fatality and he left the scene."

"What does that mean?"

"He could go to prison if he's found guilty. Wouldn't matter that he didn't hit the person. Being an accessory is treated the same way. It's a serious charge."

"How long would he be in prison?"

"Something like this could get him several years. Was there anyone else with him?"

"I don't know," she said. "I couldn't see. It was dark."

She sounds a little nervous, Lam thought.

"Well, if there was anyone else that person would be in danger of facing the same charge," he said gravely. "Both of them could wind up doing prison time. Record like that sticks with you for the rest of your life, too. Makes it harder to get a job or even a place to live."

He let that sink in for a couple of seconds.

"Now I want to tell you something and I advise you not to hang up. But first, do you know that telephone calls can be traced? We can find out the phone's number and what time the call was made."

He didn't add that it's not the easiest thing to get done and it can take next to forever to hear back from the phone company.

"Here's what I'm talking about, I don't believe that you've been completely truthful, which could put you in an awkward position to say the least. This is a serious matter. So you're more than welcome to start over."

Hearing no click of the receiver being put down, he continued.

"And if you cooperate with me and be completely honest with everything from now on, then there's a good chance nothing will happen to you. The district attorney can be very understanding in cases like this. In fact, I would even expect there would be no charges brought against you at all. Do you understand what I'm saying?"

"Yes," a small voice answered.

"Good, then let's begin with you giving me your name."

"Ke-ke Greenlaw."

~~~

"The only thing left is to make a deal with Pepe," Albert said. "I'd hoped I could find another source but it didn't work out. Actually, I never had that much faith in the whole idea from the beginning."

"You want me talk with him again?" Tiny asked.

They were in the living room. Albert had called him after returning from the airport. He hadn't expected him to arrive so soon but now he was glad that he had.

"Yes. This time tell him I have an interesting business offer for him to consider. I'd like him to join me in a partnership. Use that term, Tiny. Partnership. That'll get his attention even more so. Say that he and I need to meet and work out the details. But not at his bar. He'd take that for having control. And certainly not here at my home. I don't want him in this house. I suggest a neutral ground, perhaps the little park at the harbor. That would look like everything is in the open. Set it up for today, Tiny. We can't wait."

Chapter 28

"So the bottom line is we have a bonafide witness, Joe."

Curtis Lam had finished interviewing Ke-ke Greenlaw. She'd begrudgingly agreed to come into the station. He had called Joe afterwards to fill him in.

"Did she tell you why she'd waited until now to say anything?" Joe asked.

"I didn't push her on that but my guess is she wanted some payback for being dumped by the boyfriend and saw the story as an opportunity. Didn't realize she'd be dragged into it along with him."

"Walt is going to be surprised when he hear this," Joe chuckled. "He's taking off a couple of vacation days. And she positively identified Olomano as the driver?"

"The VW was in the lane beside them at the stoplight. She was in the passenger seat. She and Olomano even exchanged looks. How lucky was that? She ID'd him from the photo I showed her. He beat the truck through the intersection, which was his and Ricola's bad luck."

"How soon are you taking it to the Prosecuting Attorney for filing?"

"First thing in the morning. I'm staying late to write the report. Try to get an arrest warrant on Olomano signed off by the judge at the same time. Want to come with me on the arrest?"

"Absolutely. Shall I try to get in touch with Walt? He'd probably like to be there, too."

"Nah, let him enjoy himself. Two of us should be enough to handle this kid."

"What about the truck driver. You going to get a felony filing on him, too?"

"Have to think about that, Joe. Could become a problem. I'm going to talk with the PA after I make a run for not charging the witness as an accessory. This might sound shitty but it could be to everyone's benefit to reduce the charge to a misdemeanor and let him walk."

"Why? He's an accessory to a damn felony."

"I know that but the witness is afraid of the guy. Seems he fancies himself as being a badass. The type of creep some women seem to fall for, you know? She says he might beat her up if he finds out she ratted on him. I'm going to see if he has any kind of record. If he's clean, maybe the Prosecuting Attorney will work out a deal and make everybody happy. End it right there."

"So stick his ass in jail for hit-and-run and threatening a witness," Joe argued back. "That's a better ending in my opinion."

"Maybe so but look at it this way," Curtis said. "Suppose he does go down on this. He gets a lawyer and denies everything. Claims she's lying and set him up because he split on her. That's half true, not her lying but the revenge part. That could throw some doubt on her as a reliable witness. Olomano's lawyer would jump on it in a minute. If it went to court, who knows what would happen? Jurors can be funny."

"I'm not sure that'd cut any ice with the evidence you have, Curtis. But if he does have to get a lawyer, they might try to play that card. Still, I don't think it would make any difference. But you're right, why take the chance? I agree that everything would go a lot smoother if you can leave her out and just rub his nose in it with the misdemeanor. If the guy has any brains at all, he'll be thankful."

"We'll have to leave it up to the PA."

~ ~ ~

Pepe Tanaka had agreed to meet with Albert, but not at the park as had been suggested. He'd insisted Albert come to the Mongoose instead. More so, that he come alone. Albert had balked at first but Pepe had held fast. In the end, Albert had conceded to Pepe's demand.

To Albert, losing the park location had been a slight setback. He'd felt it gave Pepe an edge. He'd also felt uneasy about the whole arrangement, considering Pepe's reputation for violence. He'd even toyed with the idea of arming himself with George's old pistol that his brother had kept from his stint with the sheriffs department. He'd passed on that idea since he'd never fired a gun in his life and might possibly wind up shooting himself. Instead, he had brought along Tiny.

The bar was empty when they entered. Pepe sat at his favorite table near the rear of the room.

"You must not hear too good, old man," Pepe smirked when he saw Tiny. "What's he doing here? I said for you to come alone."

"He's here to make sure I stay an old man," Albert retorted. "Tiny can sit here up front."

"Uh-uh, he can sit out front in the car. Otherwise you both can go the fuck home."

Albert gave him a smirk of his own.

"Then you would've missed what I have to say. But all right. Wait in the car, Tiny. But keep the windows down."

Tiny left and Albert joined Pepe at the table.

"You think that old lard ass is going to be much help?" Pepe laughed harshly. "He'll probably turn on the radio as soon as he gets in the car. Have to turn in up loud since he's probably half deaf. Now, what's this about?"

"It's about making both of us rich," Albert said smoothly. "Wealthier beyond your wildest dreams. Interested?"

Chapter 29

"Maui? When did you go?"

"This afternoon," Lillian said. "A little problem popped up that demanded my attention. The client's needy that way."

"Gee, I was hoping to see you tonight," Joe said.

"I was hoping to see you, too."

"When do you think this little problem will be solved?"

"Everyone thinks we should be finished by tomorrow afternoon but don't plan on it. Could go into the next day."

"I'll cross my fingers for tomorrow."

"Me, too. There's another thing that's kind of disturbing. Mom called me. Dad's sick again"

"I'm sorry. How serious?"

"She didn't say. I've a feeling that it's not too bad. Still a worry, though. Everyone thought he'd beat that crap he picked up in Viet Nam once and for all the last time. Guess it's never going to go completely away."

The US military's defoliation program during the war used a herbicide called Agent Orange which was sprayed from airplanes and which later proved disastrous to the many soldiers and civilians who'd been exposed to it, resulting in cancers and other serious illnesses.

"Would you like to see them? I can try to get another compassionate leave and go with you."

"I know they'd like for me to come. And thank you for offering to come with me. It's just that Florida is on the other side of the world. They only moved there after he retired because it was a cheaper place to live. Should've stayed here. I could have helped them out."

"Yeah, Florida is a long way from here but from what I understand Tampa is a nice place to live. They were smart to think about their money. Army doesn't pay all that much when you retire, even after serving thirty years. No raises, either."

"I suppose you're right and they wouldn't have stood for me giving them anything. And then there's the damn project I'm working on, Joe. The way things are moving I can't afford to get behind again. I know that sounds selfish but I have to consider it."

"We'll talk about it when you get back."

"Okay," she said. "Love you."

She hung up.

Joe replaced his phone in the cradle and thought about his father-in-law.

The two of them had spent a lot of time in those same jungles. So how did he escape getting sick? Just luck of the draw. Defoliation. Kill the trees so the enemy wouldn't have any place to hide. What a dumb idea that had been. They could still shoot at you, leaves or not. It was just one more step in ruining a country and bringing more misery to its people. What went on in Viet Nam only made sense to the insane. Insanity was the reality. At least, the government was finally doing something about helping out those who were there. But where did that leave his father-in-law today? And everyone else who's in the same boat with him? Questions leading to nowhere and offering nothing other than a reminder of a war that shouldn't have happened.

He wondered how Curtis Lam was coming along on his report. Maybe he should give him a call. He started to pick up his phone but changed his mind. He suddenly felt tired. He decided to make it an early night instead.

~~~

Detective Lam was at the Prosecuting Attorney's Office at nine sharp the next morning. The man hadn't gotten in yet. He took a seat in the waiting area outside of his office. Thirty minutes later he showed up, checked with his secretary about his schedule and shot a look at Lam.

"Sorry to be late, detective," he said. "What a nightmare morning. The shower plugged up, the toilet overflowed and the plumber can't come before noon. It's enough to piss off a saint. Hope you have something good. Come in."

Curtis followed him into his office and stood while he fussed at some papers lying on his desk top before sitting.

"Okay, let's have it," he said.

"This is a report on a fatal hit-and-run that took place in Chinatown," Curtis explained, removing the document from his briefcase and handing it to him. "I have a bonafide witness to the incident. I'd like to get a felony filing on the driver of the car involved and I need to talk with you about the witness."

"Talk about what?"

"Dropping any possible charges against her."

"That's a very interesting proposal considering I don't know what she's done. Have a seat, detective."

~~~

"Get up and get dressed, Kedron," Teresa Olomano said urgently.

She stood in the bedroom at the doorway. Kedron was lying in bed with the covers pulled over his head,

"Huh?" he muttered from beneath.

"I said to get out of bed and put your damn clothes on!" she repeated, angry this time. "And hurry. We don't have much time."

"What's happening?" he asked, tossing back the covers and sitting up.

"The police are coming. I've called Sterling. I only hope he can get here first. Your father is going to be so embarrassed."

"Why are the police coming?"

"To take you to jail, you foolish boy, that's why. Quit wasting time and do what I said!"

She turned and stormed out.

~~~

"It was beautiful," Curtis Lam said.

He and Joe Cheo were driving to Diamond Head. He'd stopped by the station to pick up Joe after leaving the Prosecuting Attorneys Office.

"The PA went along with our idea of not charging the witness but still wants to think about letting off the boyfriend. Might be a step too far. Judge Elliot Farge was in the building so I got him to sign the arrest warrant. Funny, he was a little reluctant at first. Asked if we were being too hasty. I assured him that everything was solid and we needed to move fast."

"I agree with the PA on the boyfriend," Joe said. "Frankly, both of them should go down as accessories. Maybe her not as much as him since she wasn't driving but she saw what happened and kept her mouth shut."

"Well, now we're going to get the main character in this show. Just hope he's home. Fancy neighborhood, huh?"

The houses along the street were expansive and expensive. Money run amuck.

"It should be just up ahead," he said.

A botanical garden looking very much like a manicured rain forest blocked any view of the house. Joe figured his total paycheck just might handle the gardener's fee.

A car was parked in front of the house. They drove past and pulled in.

Curtis checked the house number, which was on a bronze plate set in a huge basalt stone to the side of the gate. A speaker was positioned below the plate. He pushed the button.

No answer. He pressed again, holding it longer this time.

"Who is it?" a female voice replied.

"This is Detective Curtis Lam from the Honolulu Police Department. I spoke with someone here earlier. Please open the gate."

Another moment passed and the gate buzzed unlocked. The two detectives made their way up the row of palms that lined the walk to the front door. It was open and Teresa Olomano and Sterling Huddleston stood in the doorway.

"He's not here," Teresa told them tearfully. "He took his father's car."

~~~

The old station wagon cut in and out of traffic on the H-1 east past Kahala to where it becomes the Kamehameha Highway heading north. Speeding past Mokoli'i Island, shaped like a Chinaman's hat resting up to its brim in Kaneohe Bay, it continued on to the North Shore.

Kedron wrestled the old wagon through a series of turns and barreled ahead. He imagined his father sitting in the passenger seat nervously jamming on the brakes and yelling at him to slow down. He laughed at the thought.

His old man will be pissed off royally that he'd taken his precious car. He'll leave the key in the ignition when he dumps the piece of junk. Maybe someone will steal it.

He still can't believe the fucking cops were coming to arrest him. How did his mom know that? She had to have been out of her skull if she thought he would wait around. And that dumbass lawyer she called. What could that jerk do? Well, he certainly did something himself, didn't he. Got dressed and split. He'd stay with some buddies on the North Shore.

Turning off the main highway and onto a secondary road, he pushed the wagon even harder. Sweeping into a sharp off-camber curve at high speed, the rear end breaks loose and starts to come around as the tires lose traction. He counter steered and floored the accelerator but the six-cylinder engine is already at its limits and there's not enough oomph left to recover from the spin. The wagon hit the berm sideways and flipped over twice, finally coming to rest upside down in the middle of a taro pond in a wooded area.

Chapter 30

"Who told you we were coming, ma'am?" Joe asked.

Teresa Olomano looked helplessly at Sterling Huddleson.

"That's privileged information, detective," Sterling Huddleson answered for her. "I can't reveal the source."

"It's possible someone has broken the law," Curtis Lam cautioned.

They were all in the living room at the house.

"I don't believe you will find that to be the case," Huddleson replied.

"I called Sterling to come here," Teresa Olomano said. "It's my son that we're talking about."

"Kedron needed representation in this situation," Huddleson continued. "As the family's lawyer, it was my duty to assist. I can assure you there was no intention of not complying with the warrant. He would have willingly gone with you. We are both surprised and disappointed. You can imagine how frightened the boy must have been to have taken that course. Our concern now is for his well-being."

"You are right to be concerned, Mr. Huddleson," Curtis told her. "And so is Kedron. This little stunt he's pulled makes him a fugitive. That's another ballgame. Have you any idea of where he might've gone, Mrs. Olomano? Does he have any friends? Special places? Things like that?"

"I've always tried to give him his privacy," she sniffled. "Stay out of his business. You know how young people can be."

"All right," Curtis said. "We'll leave it at that. Should he call you, find out where he is and tell him he needs to come in. I can't stress the importance of that enough, ma'am. About the car he took. You said it was your husband's?"

"Yes, it's an old station wagon. Orange with a white top. I don't know the make. I'm not all that familiar with automobiles."

"Do you have the registration card here?"

"No, I would imagine it's in the car."

" I don't suppose you would know the license number."

"I don't even know my own car's license, detective," she laughed, nervously.

"We can get it from DMV. We'll put out a be-on-the-lookout request. Hopefully, someone will spot it.

"What will happen when you find him?"

"We'll arrest him," Curtis told her.

~~~

Helen Cheo had taken the long walk down the rutted dirt road to the Hauoli Grocery store to mail a letter in the late afternoon. She enjoyed the walk and felt it did her good.

Last night she'd heard a pueo call from near the house and wondered if it was nesting or merely hunting. It was of no concern today because she had been walking and had the bird remained and decided to fly in front of her it would have brought her good luck. Had she been riding in anything, even on a horse, it would've meant bad luck.

There are two kinds of owls in Hawaii. The white Hawaiian Owl is native and endangered. It is revered and a symbol of luck. It can also be a family's 'aumakua, a god to guide them through life.

The other owl is the common barn owl which was introduced to the islands and has no influence.

Most people now consider this as just one more superstition, along with others such as not to walk under a certain tree because an 'Old One' might be lurking there. She would warn the delivery boy who always rode his bike along the road to be careful, however.

She looked at the envelope once more to make sure she'd addressed it correctly and had put on the right amount of stamps, then she deposited it in the mailbox. She spoke to the grocer about the pueo before leaving for her journey back to the Robinsons. But she must hurry now if she is to get home before dark.

~~~

Curtis and Joe arrived at the police station in the middle of shift change. Joe said he'd stick around while Curtis checked with DMV for the license plate number on the station wagon. It didn't take very long to get the information.

"Here we go," Curtis said. "1960 Ford Falcon wagon registered to Louis Olomano. License number 42013. Boy, that plate goes back a ways. I'll put out a BOLO."

"Guess he didn't go in for vanity plates," Joe commented.

"Wonder what it would have been?" Curtis smiled.

"Give me a call when you get something," Joe said. "I'm going home."

Joe left the station but instead of driving straight home he stopped by his own station to see if there was anything he needed to know. He was surprised to find Walt Douglas sitting at his desk.

"Thought you were on vacation," he said.

"I was but I found some more evidence on those burglaries I wanted to file. What I had wasn't strong enough for any more than a misdemeanor. Maybe I can step it up to a felony now. What's been happening with you?"

"Not much," Joe said casually. "Kedron Olomano was moved up to fugitive status. That boy's going places, I tell you."

Then he took Walt through the events of the day.

"Who tipped them off?" Walt asked when he'd finished.

"Lam said he got the arrest warrant signed off as soon as the Prosecuting Attorney filed. Judge Farge was available to do the honors. I might drop by there, maybe see what's what."

"Good luck with that," Walt said. "Everything's becoming CYA. Cover your ass."

"Don't I know it," Joe agreed.

"Sterling Huddleson being there when you arrived was interesting," Walt said.

"The mom said she called him. Wonder who called her?"

"Huddleson always impressed me as being kind of slick. You find that to be so about him?"

"Yeah, he's even slicker now," Joe said. "But he did a good job when he was with the City Attorney so I really can't complain. He's just doing what he's supposed to do."

"You're too forgiving," Walt said. "Anyone ever tell you that?"

"All the time," Joe laughed. "Ask Lillian. Which reminds me, I'd better call and see if she's home. She was hoping to finish that thing in Maui."

He grabbed his desk phone and dialed her number. The answering machine picked up.

"Hi, it's me. Guess it's going to be another day. Love you."

He gave Walt a little smile and left for his apartment.

Chapter 31

The next day broke dark and sullen in a heavy downpour, the rain unrelenting all morning. Detective Curtis Lam had gotten in to the station late and discovered he'd just missed a phone call. He saw it was important and immediately returned it.

"This is Detective Sugawara," the caller answered.

"Good morning, detective. I'm Detective Curtis Lam. You called me about the BOLO?"

"Yes, traffic found your car in a taro pond near Mililani. Thought you might want to be there when we pull it out."

The drive to the North Shore took about forty five minutes in the rain, which had finally begun to slacken. Lam had stopped to pick up Joe at his station. Lieutenant Ito hadn't been in his office so there'd been no problem with him leaving. He'd signed out anyway.

"That must be it," Joe said.

A squad car was parked on the side of the road up ahead with its roof rack lights flashing. Lam pulled in. Farther over and near the tree line a couple more cars and a towing truck were parked. After showing his credentials to the officer in the squad car, Lam drove down to them and parked.

Four men stood at the edge of a taro pond. One was a uniformed police officer and the others were in civilian clothes. A vehicle could be seen turned upside down in the middle of the pond.

"Good morning, gentlemen," Lam called to the group, as he and Joe got out of the car. "I'm Detective Curtis Lam and this is Detective Joe Cheo."

"I'm Detective Gary Sugawara," a man wearing a sport coat and a Hawaiian shirt. "And this is Officer Tim Kane. He answered the initial call."

Kane smiled and tipped his finger as a salute.

The other two men introduced themselves as being with the tow truck.

"Well, there's your car," Sugawara said, pointing to the half-sunken Ford Falcon.

"What about the driver?" Lam asked.

"Officer Kane said the car was empty when he arrived."

"I waded out to it," Kane explained. "I keep a set of fishing waders in my car's trunk. Comes in handy sometimes. The driver's side door was open but no one was inside."

"Who called it in?" Joe asked.

"Farmer who owns the pond." Sugawara said. "Lives nearby. He came out see how his taro plants were doing. This is a pretty big pond. All this rain we've had lately could ruin them. They're shallow-rooted and are just planted near the edge. Doesn't take much to wash them out of the ground. Then they just sink in the deeper water and die. He was going to drain off some water if he had to. He saw the car and called us."

"Does he pump out the water?" Lam asked.

"Don't need a pump for this sort of thing, not that he has one anyway," Kane said. "Just dig a couple little trenches off to the side. That'd drain out enough to keep the plants safe. But I think he's got a bigger problem with the gas and gunk from the car getting in the water and killing his plants."

"How long would it take to drain the entire pond?" Lam asked. "Driver's body could be on the bottom."

"We could bring a pump out here," Sugawara suggested "Might take all day and half the night to completely empty it. Have to talk with the farmer. He might not be too happy about doing that. Ruin his plants for sure."

"How deep was the water out there when you were wading around?" Joe asked Kane.

"Three feet or so where the car is," he said. "Waders are chest high. No problem."

"You wouldn't have an extra set of waders would you, Tim?" Joe asked

"Just the one."

"Tell you what, Tim, get back in your waders and I'll take off my pants and shoes. You and I can go out there and have a look around."

He could be under the car," Kane offered.

"That'll be the last place we look after they drag it out," Joe said, kicking off his shoes and removing his trousers.

On second thought, he decided to replace his shoes for safety and laced them tight. You don't know what might be on the bottom.

Like farmers wading in a rice paddy, the two cops began to duckwalk through the flooded pond. Tangles of roots pulled at Joe's legs and he nearly lost one of his shoes. The only thing they found for all of their effort was an old rifle that'd appeared to have been there for ages. Its barrel was hopelessly corroded. What was probably once a handsome walnut stock had been reduced to a piece of black rotted wood.

"Looks like a Winchester lever-action," Sugawara said when they'd given to him. "Except the lever is missing."

"My dad owned one of those," Joe mentioned. "Winchester 30-30. Best pig shooting rifle ever, he'd said."

"Probably should send it to ballistics," Sugawara said. "Be a waste of time, on the other hand. Shape it's in there'd not be anything usable on it now. You say your dad had a riffle like this? Why don't you keep it then. Just going to be trashed anyway."

Joe was surprised by the offer.

"Think I will," he said.

"Let's get that wreck pulled out," Sugawara told the truck operators.

The two men hooked a cable to the Ford's rear axle, gears engaged and the wagon began to slowly slide from the pond. No body was revealed lying beneath it.

"If we can get it upright, can you tow it to the impound yard?" Sugawara asked. "Or do we need a flatbed?"

"We can flip it over on its wheels," one of the men said. "No problem. Tow it to the yard, too."

Soon the old Ford staton wagon had regained its footing and was wenched nose up in back of the truck and secured. Water continued to drain out of the back as they drove away.

Sugawara said he would copy Lam with his report. Lam thanked everyone and he and Joe left for Honolulu, Joe's soggy shoes tied to the sideview mirror to dry flopping in the wind, the old Winchester rifle lying on the rear seat.

"I'm going home to change clothes after you drop me off," Joe said. "Probably go back to the office. Call me there if anything turns up."

"I'll get out another BOLO on Olomano at nightshift's role call," Lam said. "Personally, I don't understand why the kid didn't get killed."

"He might've gotten hurt," Joe said. "Be good to check with any clinics around here."

"Yeah, I'll be on that."

"You going to call the family?"

"That, too."

~~~

Albert and Pepe were at the Mongoose Bar. After giving some thought to Albert's earlier offer to join him in the casino investment scheme, Pepe had decided to take it. The decision hadn't been easy for either one. Pepe having ripped off the drugs was a bitter issue with Albert but he could visit with that later. Getting them back and on the market to sell was the matter at hand. Pepe didn't trust Albert but understood he had more to gain by going in with him than trafficking in the drugs himself. Money is a great compromiser. Now they were meeting to go over the details. Tiny waited out front in the car.

The conversation had returned to the night the drugs were taken.

'Somebody else was in on it and Frank switched the keys with him," Pepe said. 'Cause he didn't go back into that locker room after we'd stored the drugs."

"Frank could've had two keys all along and purposely gave you the wrong one," Albert shrugged. "Wouldn't have been a hard thing to do."

Though painful to sit here and listen to how he had been taken for a fool in this, there was some pleasure in hearing that he wasn't alone. They were right about there being no honor among thieves, he thought.

"He had only one key on him," Pepe said.

Albert gave him a quizzical look. He almost had to laugh. Does this idiot realize what he'd just said? He's admitted to killing Frank. How else would he have known there was only one key, which indeed had turned out to belong to another locker. But he's right about someone else being involved. Frank had obviously rented two lockers. Palmed off the real one at some point. Planned to return to the bar and get the drugs after he'd dropped off Pepe. The double-crosser had been doubled-crossed himself and it'd cost him his life. However, that did nothing to help with the present situation.

"If another person was involved, he most likely has the drugs now," he said.

"There's no action on the street, Albert. I have sources, too. I've checked it out. Those drugs are still in the other locker."

"And your plan is to go back to this Asterisk bar with Tiny and the two of you threaten the bartender or whoever's there to make him open the locker," Albert said. "Might be a better idea to let a thousand dollars do the talking. Nobody turns down easy money."

Pepe smirked.

"I'll ask politely at first, if that makes you feel any better."

"I'm trying to be reasonable," Albert said. "We can't afford trouble. This is the only chance we'll get. Don't you understand?"

"There won't be any trouble," Pepe answered hotly. "Lard ass is coming along for show. His size will scare the shit out of that bartender. I'll have lard ass crack his knuckles or growl at him. Place opens at eleven. We'll be there right when he's unlocking the door. Shove him inside and lock up again. We'll be in the back room, we'll be out of sight. Anybody tries to come in they'll think the bar hasn't opened. We can take the first plane out tomorrow. Get the next one back soon as we're done."

"All right," Albert said. "But once you have the drugs, forget about coming back with them on the airplane. They're checking for drugs at the airport. That's been in the paper for the past two days. They've even got dogs sniffing for them. It's too risky."

Pepe huffed a breath.

"So let's rent a private plane," he said. "Don't have to go through the fucking terminal."

"They're checking at that part of the airport, too. The safest thing is to take the tug and barge back. It leaves Pearl Harbor for Hilo tomorrow afternoon. I'll make arrangements for you and Tiny to be on it. Go straight to the docks after you finish with the bar."

"I'm not comfortable on boats," Pepe complained. "They make me sick. Starts as soon as I step on the fucking things. Can't help it."

Albert liked the thought of him getting seasick.

"Suck on a lemon," he said. "It's a sure cure. I'll have Tiny pick up a bag of them. And stay up on deck. Fresh air helps, too."

And a mid-channel swim on the return trip would be a surer cure for everything, he thought to himself. He'd speak to Tiny about that.

~ ~ ~

Joe had hung around the station until the role call for nightshift. The BOLO for Olomano had be read to patrol. However, he hadn't heard anything from Lillian during the whole time. The detective's not calling had only meant there was nothing new to report. Lillian's, though, had begun to worry him.

Before leaving he tried calling her once more. And again her machine had answered.

When he got home, he saw there was a message waiting on his machine.

'Joe, I have to go to Florida. Dad's taken a turn for the worse. I tried reaching you at the station but was told you'd signed out for the day. I'll call as soon as I learn anything. I love you.'

That had come more than six hours ago. He hadn't checked his messages when he'd stopped by earlier to change clothes. Why the hell hadn't someone left him a note at work that she'd called? Did she call from the airport? She's probably in California or on the way to Florida by now.

He looked at his watch. There's a five-hour time difference between them. It was too late to call her folks there. He'd have to wait until tomorrow.

Should he go ahead and make an airline reservation for the next flight he could get? No, he really did need to first find out what was actually going on. He played the message again. And then turned in for what would probably be a sleepless night.

Chapter 32

Joe's telephone rang at 4:15 a.m., startling him awake. He fumbled for the phone on the bedside table.

"Yeah?" he answered sleepily.

"Joe, it's me."

"Lillian? Where are you? I didn't get your message until late last night."

He sat up on the side of the bed and switched on the lamp.

"I'm in Miami. My flight to Tampa leaves in thirty minutes. I've been flying since yesterday."

"Have you spoken with your folks, yet?"

"Yes, dad's feeling better. At least, he said he was. Mom's still a mess."

"I'll come as soon as I can. Shouldn't be any problem. Okay?"

"Let me call you after I get there and find out more. It may not be as serious as it sounded at first. I have to run now. Love you."

"Love you, too."

There was no use trying to go back to sleep. Actually, he felt pretty well-rested considering. He must've drifted off as soon as he hit the pillows. He got up and slipped on a pair of shorts and a teeshirt.

First light wouldn't be for another hour. He made a pot of coffee and took it out on the balcony to wait for sunrise.

The city was already up.

Faint traffic noises, lights on in some buildings, a sense of energy beginning to build.

He thought of his father-in-law. Lillian had said he sounded better. Or was he putting a good face on a bad situation? It would be just like him to do that.

A patrol car sped down the street below and stopped in the next block where two officers stood on the sidewalk with a man in custody. Joe looked wistfully at the scene and turned to go back inside.

The sun peaked over the mountains, brightening Honolulu in a new day.

~~~

Pepe and Tiny were buckled in their seats aboard the Aloha Airlines jet scheduled to depart Hilo for Honolulu at 7:40 a.m. They sat across the aisle opposite from each other, Pepe wanting a little more elbow room. The main cabin door had been closed and the airplane had started its engines but still hadn't left the gate.

Then the engines shut down.

A hush quickly spread throughout the cabin followed by a few groans.

Tiny looked over at Pepe.

"What the fuck?" Pepe said a little too loudly, which got him a frown from the flight attendant.

An announcement came over the speakers.

"Folks, this is the captain. We have a little electrical problem. Should be fixed soon. Don't expect it to delay us much."

A few minutes later, the flight attendant opened the door and two maintenance men came in and went to the cockpit.

~~~

Albert had prepared a small breakfast and had taken it into the living room of the ohana where he had been staying since Helen had gone to Kauai. It offered more privacy than the main house. He was still getting the occasional knock on the front door from well-wishers even though George was long in the ground.

He was feeling chipper this morning.

By late tomorrow night he should have the drugs. They'd be on the street the next day. And by his reckoning, he should be more than able to meet Louis Olomano's piratical price to join the partnership.

Perhaps now would be a good time to call Louis. He rubbed his hands together and picked up his phone.

"Good morning, Louis," he said brightly. "Albert Cheo here. Hope I didn't awaken you."

"Who is this again?"

"Albert Cheo. Wanted you to know that I'll be in a position to buy a share within a couple of days. Save me one before they all are sold. Or maybe I'll take two, ha, ha."

"Call me when you have the money, Mr. Cheo. Now, something has come up and I'm very busy."

"Anything I can help you with, Louis?"

The dial tone replied.

~~~

"Mom took him to the VA hospital," Lillian said. "They told him to get some rest. No need to change his medication. Blah, blah, blah."

Joe was watching the morning news on television when Lillian called. He hadn't gotten dressed for work. He wasn't sure whether he would be going to the station or the airport.

"Typical VA," he said.

"Typical bullshit to me," Lillian replied.

"You think he should see someone else? The VA is pretty knowledgable on herbicide poisoning but it probably wouldn't be a bad idea to get another opinion."

"He doesn't have a regular doctor. I told him he should have one. Know what he said about that? He said Uncle Sam was good enough for thirty years so why would he want to change now?"

Joe laughed.

"Why am I not surprised?"

"Maybe you can talk some sense into him. He's right here. Hold on."

Joe pictured the two of them sitting there five thousand miles away.

"Hello, Joe. How're things in sunny Hawaii?"

"Same as probably in Florida. Sunny and hot. What's going on, Bill? This isn't something you mess around with."

"No need to start digging any holes just yet, Joe. Had a little flareup. It's gone now. Nothing that hasn't happened before."

"Lillian believes you should see another doctor. I'm all for that. Second opinion wouldn't hurt."

"Joe, all the opinions in the world aren't going to change a damn thing. I know that. And you know that. It is what it is and we just have to accept it. Here's a crazy thing. I was thinking the other day about those three VCs we captured. The ones that ARVN son of a bitch shot, remember that?"

"Hard to forget."

"Don't know why it came to mind. Having a lot of memories lately. But it made me wonder how many names we kept off the Wall that day."

"I'd say more than a few."

"Then we made a good swap. You take care of yourself, Joe. I'll put Lillian back on."

"Now you know what I'm up against," she said tiredly.

"Would you like for me to come? I still have some vacation time."

"No, but thanks for asking. I'm going to talk with mom. If she's okay, I'll get out of here tomorrow morning. There's really nothing more I can do."

"All right, let me know your flight. I'll meet you at the airport. Love you."

"Love you, too."

Joe stepped out on the balcony. The traffic on the street below had grown heavier, the sidewalks fuller. Beyond toward the ocean, he could hear the beckoning surf at Waikiki. He went back inside and dressed for work.

Chapter 33

"I'll make certain they note that you're coming in voluntarily, Kedron," Sterling Huddleson said.

Kedron had been dropped off at his home earlier by a friend. He didn't tell his parents the friend's name or where he'd been the night before. He had a goose-egg size bump on his forehead. After he had cleaned up and changed clothes, they had called Huddleson. Now they were all assembled in the living room.

"Will they put him in jail?" Teresa Olomano asked tearfully.

"Maybe that would teach him a lesson," Louis Olomano huffed angrily.

"Stop it, Louis! He's just a boy."

"It's possible," Huddleson said. "He will be arrested. I realize this is upsetting but…"

"Upsetting isn't the half of it, Sterling," Louis Olomano interrupted. "Do you realize how this will look? It could get in the papers. There's a great deal at stake at the moment. I had a potential investor call me right before you arrived."

Huddleson took a breath before replying.

"I was about to say Kedron's turning himself in on his own volition will, to address your concern, look better than if he'd been picked up by the police. How this could affect your investors, I can't say."

"Can't he just pay a fine?" Teresa asked. "It wasn't like he hit that man on purpose. It was an accident."

"I"m sure it was an accident. The problem is he didn't stop. For now, if he's arrested, hopefully bail will be set at the booking. Otherwise, he'll have to wait until the arraignment, which could be days later. I'll talk with the prosecuting attorney about speeding things up should that happen."

"How much will the bail cost?" Louis asked.

"They have a pre-set amount for minor misdemeanors, which is generally taken care of when a person is booked, but this is more serious. I understand he hasn't any priors, so that's a help."

Of course he wouldn't, Huddleson thought, Judge Farge always quashed them.

"And what about my car?" Louis asked. "Where's it?"

"I would imagine it was taken to the impound. I'll try to find out where. Are you ready to go, Kedron?"

Kedron nodded. He hadn't said much since Huddleson arrived.

"Good. Teresa, I'd like Kedron to ride with me to the police station. You and Louis follow us in your car."

~~~

The 7:40 from Hilo to Honolulu had wheels up by 9:30. Just under an hour later the airplane was parked at the gate in Honolulu International and all of its disgruntled passengers had disembarked.

Pepe and Tiny had taken a cab and were on the way to the Asterisk.

"Did you see any cops in the airport looking at bags?" Pepe asked. "I didn't see a fucking one."

"Maybe they weren't wearing their uniforms so you couldn't tell," Tiny offered.

"Tells me there's no need for us to take that fucking boat back," Pepe said.

"The captain knows we're coming. Albert arranged everything. I think we better go on it."

"Yeah? Well, you take it. I'm flying back. And the stuff"s coming with me. Oh, and you can keep your fucking lemons."

Tiny started to protest but decided to keep quiet for the moment.

"Fuck, look at the time," Pepe said bitterly, checking his watch. "We're going to be late. Hey, driver, step on it, will you?"

"Should be in the next block, sir."

"Okay, we won't be there long," Pepe told him. "Wait for us."

"I have to get back to the airport, sir."

"So do we," Pepe said, handing him a hundred dollar bill. "There'll be another one for you at the airport."

The cab passed the Asterisk, swung a u-turn and parked in front.

"Here we are, sir."

"Don't go anywhere," Pepe told the driver, getting out.

"We're too late," Tiny said anxiously." It's already open."

They went in. The bar was empty but they could hear someone rustling around in back.

A moment later Keanu appeared.

"Good morning," he said, going behind the bar. "What can I get you?"

"Remember me?" Pepe grinned.

Keanu squinted and then nodded.

"Yeah, I remember you," he said. "You claimed somebody stole something from your locker. Raised all kinds of hell, going to tear up the place, right? We called the cops on you, pal. Too bad you left before they got here."

Pepe exchanged the grin for one more menacing.

"I was smart to leave then, asshole, because I knew I could come back. And you should be smart this time and open every one of those lockers for me."

"Can't do that."

Pepe laughed.

"Tiny, show this stupid fuckhead why he'd better do that."

Tiny took in a deep breath, which made him look even larger, and started to move around the bar.

"Okay, take it easy," Keanu said, raising his hands palms out. "I'll get the master key."

He reached beneath the bar, grabbed the baseball bat and swung it hard, hitting Tiny square across the chest.

Tiny stumbled backwards barely managing to keep his balance. The next swing caught Pepe high on the shoulder, clipping his jaw and sending him to the floor.

"Get the hell out of here!" Keanu yelled, gripping the bat like he was ready to hit a homer out of the park.

Tiny helped Pepe get to his feet.

"Move it!" Keanu shouted, prodding them along with the bat.

They made their way to the door and Keanu shoved them out to the sidewalk.

"As far as that locker goes," he said, "the cops took the shit that was inside it. Too bad again for you."

He slammed the door shut and threw the lock.

The was no taxi in sight.

~~~

"We have him waiting in an interview room," Curtis Lam said. "Seemed a little kinder than slamming him in a holding cell. His parents are here."

He had called Joe at the station to tell him that Kedron Olomano had been arrested.

"He walked in and gave himself up just like that?" Joe asked.

"Sterling Huddleson brought him in. Said he was ready to cooperate. Don't know how long he'll be here. They're talking the the PA about bail right now. He might be sent to the main jail until the arraignment if they don't come to an agreement."

"That's fantastic, Curtis. How'd he look? I mean, after having that accident. Was he injured?"

"Got a bump on his head is all. Doctor should examine him, though. Kid seemed kind of spacey to me. Maybe he's just scared. Parents are a real number. More embarrassed than anything else."

"Not surprising there," Joe said. "Thanks for calling, Curtis. I'll pass on the good news to Walt when he comes in."

Joe hung up. He probably should also bring the lieutenant into the picture since he was so concerned about sharing any solves. Make him happy. Make life better for everyone.

Lola Kahamena was erasing the latest Ito cartoon from the chalkboard when Walt Douglas walked into the detectives' room.

"Sign me in while you're at it, Lola," he said and went to his desk.

"You missed the news," Joe said. "Kedron Olomano gave himself up. Lam just called. They have him there."

"He survived the accident? Kid must carry a rabbit's foot. By the way, I'm sorry I couldn't join you and Lam. Burglary case is driving me crazy."

"He just got a knock on the noggin. Sterling Huddleson's working on bail. He'll probably get it. Doubt if they'll consider Kedron a flight risk."

"That's tremendous. Lieutenant Ito know?"

"Haven't told him. Might be better to let their captain call our captain, brass to brass, and he tells the lieutenant. We're supposed to keep a low profile, remember?"

"Ito made a big thing about sharing any solves on this thing," Walt said. "He's going to be pissed off if he misses out."

"They can figure out how to divvy it up."

"You want a cup of coffee? I'm going for one."

"Yeah, let's take it up on the roof. Need to talk with you about something."

Lola had made a fresh pot. Walt poured two cups and they went upstairs.

"You ever been to the Arizona Memorial?" Joe asked, pointing to where the ship lay.

"Ashamed to admit it but I haven't."

"You should go. My dad took me there once when I was a kid. Made an impression."

"Maybe Bee and I can plan a trip. Neither of us is from here. So what did you want to talk about?"

"Lillian's in Florida. Kind of a family emergency. Her dad wasn't doing well. She called me this morning and apparently he's better. I spoke with him. She's probably coming back tomorrow."

"That's good. What was it, his heart?"

"No, something he picked up in Viet Nam. But here's what I wanted to talk about. It was around four this morning when she called. Woke me up. I couldn't get back to sleep so I made a pot of coffee and took it out on the balcony. City's pretty that time of morning."

"I've seen it a few times then."

"Just before it started to get light, a squad car stopped on the street below me. A couple of uniforms waiting on the corner had a suspect in cuffs. They loaded him in the car. Brought back memories. Thing is, Walt, I miss that."

"So what are you saying, Joe?"

"I'm thinking of returning to patrol."

Walt set his cup of coffee down on the building's ledge.

"You're a good detective, Joe. I know Ito's a pain in the ass but he won't be here forever. He's already taken the captain's test. He's ambitious and political. Winning combination. Could be moved up any time now."

"It's not just Ito," Joe said. "I enjoy working in detectives but I was much happier in patrol. It's the front line. You did your job. And sometimes you made a difference. Nothing beats that."

"I'm not aware of anyone who switched back to patrol," Walt said. "Can it even be done?"

"It's not easy but there is a procedure. You make a request and that has to go through the chain of command all the way to the

top. It can be refused and returned at any point along the way. That's
my problem. It starts with your present supervisor. I won't even get
to first base but maybe I'll give it a try."

Walt shook his head.

"Hell, I don't want you to go," he said. "I think we work pretty
good together."

"Thanks, Walt. Me too."

~~~

"Good thing you got here when you did," the first mate said.
"Captain decided to leave early. We're about to shove off."

Unable to find a taxi, Pepe and Tiny had taken the bus to the
docks. Pepe had wanted to go to the airport but Tiny had been
afraid the barkeeper might've called the police and they'd be
watching for them. Pepe had reminded him that they hadn't seen
any cops when they arrived so there was no reason to think there'd
be any now. But Tiny had persisted and Pepe's jaw had hurt too
much to argue any further so Tiny had won in the end.

"Channel's gonna be rough the entire crossing," the first mate
explained. "You two might want to stay below if the weather picks
up."

True to his word, they began to hit heavy chop just outside
the harbor.

Chapter 34

Joe stopped at his mailbox. He hadn't checked it for two days and it was full. Sorting through the letters, which were mostly bills and advertisements, he came across one from his mother. It had a Kauai postmark. He stuck it in his pocket along with the others and went up to his apartment.

It'd been a crappy day and he was glad to be home. His talk with Walt Douglas had only left him undecided about returning to patrol. Was making the request even worth the effort? Ito would refuse to pass it on not because he wouldn't want to lose him but because it might make him look bad to the brass. It could even backfire and Ito would see to it that he's fired. The news about Kedron Olomano had been good, though. He poured himself a glass of wine and took it out on the balcony. He settled in a chair and opened his mother's letter.

It read:

To my son,

There is a story that began years back with a generous act of love. But that story was flawed by a lie.

Now it is time for the truth to be told. A man and a woman married. Children were expected but none came. The husband was approached by a neighbor who offered hanai, which as you know is the Hawaiian way of spreading the blessings of family by giving a child to those who are without. The husband and wife dismissed the idea and shortly afterwards she joyfully announced that she was pregnant. The pleased husband bragged to all of his friends. A month later and while he was away on business, she became ill. She went to a shaman who gave her herbs. She miscarried and the child was lost. She didn't tell her husband what had happened and soon stopped showing herself when nude, which he accepted as her modesty, but in actuality she had begun to wear a small pillow over her stomach beneath her clothes. When the time for birth neared, she begged her husband to let her visit a friend on another island. He granted her wish and while she was there her son was 'born'. A child is a blessing given through an act of love. That is also the principle of hanai. And though you are not of my blood, Joe, you are that blessing. With the grace in the words of the Ho'oponopono, I am sorry. Please forgive me. Thank you. I love you.

Your mother.

He put the letter down. He didn't know exactly how he felt. Had a huge weight just been lifted or was another one dropped on him? All of his life he'd been Joe Cheo of the infamous crime family. Told it was in his blood. He'd listened to the taunts while growing up. Suffered the suspicions. Had run away to the Army only to return to where he'd left. It had tagged along with him after he'd become a cop. And now?

Well, he's still Joe Cheo. But in name only.

He had been adopted. Given away, when you really think about it. But putting that aside, isn't hanai supposed to bond the two families involved? So what happened to the other one, his flesh-and-blood family? Why were they kept out of the picture? Why was it a big secret for all those years? Where are they now? And his relatives from that side? Brothers? Sisters? Cousins? He'll probably never know.

His hanai family, the half he does know, treated him well enough. He was loved as a child. Though he does recall a certain coolness in his mother after he entered his teens. His father was always distant. Oddly, Albert seemed the one closest to him. Another puzzlement.

What was the purpose of this letter? It had to be more than her conscience bothering her after all these years. He'd have to ask her and he would. But not now.

He was no longer twixt and between. Torn by two opposing forces. Not free of the past but able to let it be just that. The past. Who he is hasn't changed. Who he isn't has changed and for the better. Where he goes from here is his to choose.

He folded the letter and returned it to its envelope. The sun had dropped below the horizon and was now a footlight in the darkening sky. He refilled his glass and sat back to wait for the first star to appear.

~~~

Nearly four thousand miles away in Dallas, Texas, it was midnight and the stars had appeared hours ago. Lillian was seated at the gate in Love Field Airport. She had flown there directly from Tampa. Her next flight would take her to Los Angeles, where she'd connect for the final leg to Honolulu.

It was a brutal schedule but she'd been lucky to even get it. After talking with her mom, everyone had agreed it'd be all right for her to leave. She thought she would go the next day but out of curiosity had checked with the airline and found space available for that night. She decided to grab it while she could.

She was beat. The whole experience had been exhausting. She had a feeling it wasn't over, too. She only hoped she was wrong.

It would have been nice to have called Joe but she'd had to scramble to catch the Tampa flight. They'd be announcing boarding for this one in a few minutes. She'd have more time in Los Angeles. She could call then. Wake him up again.

She'd kill him if he called her that early. She was so looking forward to seeing Joe and getting her life back together.

It was time to board. She got in line.

~~~

Restless seas had dogged the tug from Pearl Harbor to the Alenuihaha Channel, which has the reputation of having the most treacherous water and winds in the world, where they'd set course to Hawaii.

Tiny and Pepe had remained below during the earlier portion of the trip. Now a couple of the crew members had come in to take shelter.

"It's turning into a real blow," one of them said, removing his slicker. "I'm going to the bridge."

"I'll come with you," the other said. "See what the radar says."

After they left, the tug began to rise and fall like a hobbyhorse rocking.

"I have to throw up again," Pepe announced, looking a little green.

Tiny, who was feeling none too well himself and had rather not witness the event, got to his feet. The bag of lemons he'd brought along for this very purpose had been left in the taxi.

"Let's open the door and get some fresh air," he said.

"Think it's safe?" Pepe asked worriedly. "Those guys said it was getting bad out there."

"We can just stand in the doorway. Come on. It'll do you good."

To their surprise it was relatively calm outside. The tug had changed course and was plowing headlong into the wind, providing a windbreak for the rear deck.

They cautiously stepped through the door and out onto the deck.

A spray of seawater immediately wetted their faces. The deck was eerily illuminated by the yellow stern lights. The barge loomed darkly behind, its towrope stretched tightly between the two vessels. Mountainous waves swelled all around.

Pepe went to the rail and threw up.

Then it happened.

~~~

"Man overboard!" the deckhand shouted, rushing into the bridge.

"When? Where? Who?" everyone asked at once.

"One of the passengers," the deckhand answered excitedly. "They were on the aft deck and a wave washed him over the rail."

"Bring her to dead slow," the captain ordered. "Keep the towrope tight. Mark our position and radio the Coast Guard. Request assistance."

"Shall I bring her around, Captain?" the helmsman asked. "See if we can spot him?"

"No, by the time we complete the turn, the guy could be floating in Tokyo Bay. It'll be completely dark soon. Turn on the searchlight and sweep the water."

"What about taking a life raft out to look for him?" another suggested

"I can't risk putting anyone in these seas at night" the captain said. "Where's the other passenger?"

"He's below," the deckhand said.

Chapter 35

Albert was on tenterhooks. He'd learned that the barge would be late getting in. No reason for the delay had been given other than possible rough weather. To compound his disquietude, he had heard nothing from Tiny. And if that weren't enough, Helen had just arrived from Kauai. She was unpacking in her room upstairs and would be down any minute. He went to the window and stood looking out, not for any particular reason.

"Expecting someone, Albert?" Helen asked, entering the living room.

"No," he said, turning to her. "How are the Robinsons?"

"Still as blissfully backwards as you've always believed. It was very nice being there. I did take a little side trip to Ni'ihau, as I'd mentioned I might."

"I've never been to the island."

"As you know, not everyone is allowed to come."

That had always been a sore point for Albert. The Forbidden Island is off-limits to outsiders, except by invitation and then only to a very few at that. He'd considered himself to be as much Hawaiian as anyone else. Helen, however, had grown up on Ni'ihau. She was considered a native and was welcome at any time.

"I went there for a purpose, Albert," Helen continued. "It had come time to right a wrong and I needed to speak with the kahuna and seek his help in making a Ho'oponopono. It concerned Joe."

"I'm not sure I understand what you're talking about, Helen. When was Joe wronged?"

"From the very beginning and now the words of the Ho'oponopono have been spoken and the wrong righted. Eventually, things may be moved back into balance."

~~~

Joe was waiting at the gate for Lillian's flight to arrive. The letter was tucked in his pocket. He removed it and read it again.

Should he mention this to Lillian? He wondered about that. For some reason it seemed very private, written only for him to read. Was he embarrassed by it? What a question to even ask. He stuck the letter back in his pocket.

The door to the gateway opened and passengers began to stream into the terminal. Both he and Lillian spotted each other at the same time. He ran to her and they embraced. She started to cry.

"What's wrong?" Joe asked.

"I'm just so happy to see you," she sniffled.

"Me, too," he said, hugging her tighter. "Let's get out of here. You can tell me how it was on the way home."

"Do you have to go back to work?"

"Not if I can help it."

~~~

Walt Douglas had spent half the morning with the Assistant City Attorney before coming to work.

"Coast Guard sent a notice about a man falling off a boat last night," Lola Kahemena mentioned, as he was signing in. "They're alerting all police stations."

"Really? Does it say who it was?"

"Here, read it for yourself. I've already told everybody else."

She handed him a copy of the notice.

"He fell off a tugboat towing a barge to Hilo," Douglas said. "Coast Guard says he was a passenger. Wonder if Joe knows him? Has he seen this?"

"No. He's meeting his wife at the airport. There's a message for him. Came in earlier. Maybe you'd better take a look at it."

~~~

The communication's officer at the Hilo police station had received the Coast Guard alert and had taken it to the duty sergeant.

"Should have a uniform patrol officer meet that boat," the sergeant said. "Detective might want to be there, too."

"What about informing any relatives?"

"Detective will handle that. Find out who this guy was first. Assuming he lived here."

~~~

"You nailed both of them with a baseball bat?" Walt Douglas asked in disbelief. "Bet that was an unpleasant surprise."

He was on the phone with Keanu, who had left the message for Joe.

"The big one was called 'Tiny'," Keanu laughed. "Kind of funny because he was so large. Got him first. Then I whacked the other one before he realized what was happening. Shoved them outside and locked the door."

"Was anyone waiting for them?" Walt asked, scribbling the word 'Tiny' on a notepad.

"I don't know. I also told them that the police had their dope. I don't think they'll be back. What's the need?"

"Probably won't but keep that bat handy."

~~~

211

"So you just offer up a prayer and all is forgiven?" Lillian asked. "Sounds so simple."

Joe had finished reading her Helen's letter. He'd decided on the way from the airport that he would do it after they'd gotten settled.

"Doesn't mean to say it's easy," he told her. "You have to take responsibility. Put it into practice every day. Think the right thoughts. All that. And once you commit, you can't go back. Otherwise, things might get worse. Ho'oponopono is an old Hawaiian way for forgiveness. I'm glad for her."

"Personally, I think it's a cop out. All of your life you've carried this load about your family. You got a raw deal, Joe."

"I can live with it."

"Good, then how about some lunch?"

"In or out?"

"Let's go out to some place nice. We both deserve it. I have to change first."

"I should call Walt. See what's up."

Joe dialed the station and was put through to Douglas.

"I'm bugging out for the rest of the day. Lola knows. Anything going on?"

"You had a message from that bartender at the Asterisk," Walt said. "Wanted you to call him. I called him back since you weren't coming in. Wait'll you hear what it was about."

Walt repeated the conversation he'd had with Keanu.

"Could he describe Tiny?" Joe asked.

"Just said he was huge," Walt said. "Sounds like he came along to scare the guy. Whatever, it didn't work out for them. Only other news is the Coast Guard sent an alert to all police stations about some poor bastard falling off a tugboat on its way to Hilo last night. Guy was a passenger. Didn't give his name. Hope it's not someone you know."

"I hope they find him," Joe said. "There're some big fish out there. I gotta run. See you later."

He placed the phone back in its cradle. That was curious about the Asterisk and the boat accident, he thought. The timing between the two to say the least. Not that he was one for having psychic moments but he did know a large man named Tiny and someone else involved in the tugboat business. Was it simply a coincidence or could there be a connection?

Depending on where the guy went overboard and how long they spent searching for him, that tug could possibly make it to Hilo by late evening. He'd call the department there and ask about the passenger.

"Ta-da!" Lillian said, twirling around. "I'm ready."

~~~

"Got some news about John Sutton," Madalyn Crocker said, entering Harlan Faison's office.

"Who?" Faison asked.

"You know, the big shot with mob ties from Las Vegas I told you about seeing at the Olomano party, remember?"

"Oh, yeah, that guy. He was supposed to be testing the water about the gambling bill passing."

"I was talking with a friend in the Las Vegas city attorney's office this morning and she said he's back in town."

"That's interesting," Faison said. "I read in this morning's paper that a couple of churches have come out against the bill."

"Wonder how that's affecting the odds in Vegas?"

"Certainly disappoint some people around here," Faison said.

~~~

Louis Olomano finished the third disappointing phone call he'd received in the past hour. Three investors had now backed out. He picked up the newspaper and scanned the article once more. For the life of him, he couldn't understand why the story should have caused such a panic. Churches like to protest. It's their nature.

They have a reputation to uphold. Well, maybe he was better off not having these three namby-pambies in this endeavor. He may have to lower his sights. He had already locked up the Maui property. The Hukilau Hotel in Hilo was a done deal. He'd start with those two and expand later. He could afford to be patient.

His phone rang.

Chapter 36

The uniform police officer waited on the dock while the tugboat tied up. The detective he was to meet there hadn't shown up yet. Earlier, the dock master had informed the duty sergeant at the Hilo station when the tug was due. Unfortunately, he'd called right at shift change, which had resulted in some confusion over assignments.

Both bow and stern lines had now been secured and a small gangplank laid. Some of the crew began to disembark. The police officer saw the detective come onto the dock at the far end. He walked down to meet him.

Tiny was anxious to get off the boat but had become white-knuckled-scared-to- death after spotting the cop when he stepped outside. Suddenly the man walked away. This was his chance. He went down the gangplank, turned in the opposite direction from the way the cop had gone and walked away as quickly as his fat legs would carry him.

~~~

"I didn't know the man's name," the tugboat captain said. "Or if he was from around here. He wasn't a crew member. He was what we call a pickup."

The captain was being questioned by the detective.

"Could you explain what that means?" he asked.

"Someone who needs a ride to another island. He'll do odd jobs along the way for payment. No money changes hands. It's a common practice. This fellow got on in Honolulu. He was stowing some equipment on the aft deck when a wave washed him overboard. We called the Coast Guard and searched for him but it was no use."

"Did he have any bags?"

"No, he came aboard with what he was wearing. I'm sorry as hell that it happened. Nothing anybody could do."

"Well, we won't take up any more of your time," the detective said.

He and the uniformed patrol officer left the boat. The captain picked up his telephone, its line having been connected to the dock's, and dialed.

"This is Albert Cheo," a voice answered.

"Mr. Cheo, this is Captain Randel. Afraid I have some bad news. One of the passengers you told us to accommodate was lost at sea. The Coast Guard was notified and they alerted the police, as is the custom."

"Which passenger?"

"The smaller one. Other thing is the police were just here asking about the accident. I told them he was a pickup and didn't know anything about him. I also didn't mention the other fellow. Crew has been told to keep their mouths shut."

"And what about him, the other fellow?"

"He left the boat after we docked."

"Thank you, Captain Randel."

Albert hung up, a look of relief on his face.

~~~

Tiny had taken a taxi to the airport parking lot to get his car. Pepe's car was parked next to his. The sight of it had given him a small case of the willies. He'd driven home to clean up and change clothes before going to Albert. Now he had pulled up in front of the house and was very much apprehensive of what to expect.

Albert greeted him at the door with a broad smile.

"Come in," he said. "I want to hear about everything."

~~~

Joe had stopped by the station after leaving Lillian's. He wanted to call the Hilo detective. The drowning accident was still on his mind. He dialed the Hilo station, thinking that the detective had probably gone home, but to his surprise had been put through to him.

"The captain came off a little cagey to me," the detective told him. "Very cool operator. Nothing specific about the victim. No name. Said he was a pickup. You know what that is?"

"Yeah, I've heard the term," Joe said. "Didn't have a name, huh?"

"That's right. I thought that was odd. Said the guy was stowing something on deck when it happened."

"Well, that's possible," Joe said. "Same goes for the name. They're pretty lax. He was the only passenger? No one else?"

"So he claims. There's not much more we can do. I'm sure the crew will back him up. They followed all the rules. Called the Coast Guard, maintained their position, searched as best they could. Guess that's it."

"I guess so, too," Joe said. "I appreciate your help."

"Any time. If you're ever this way, drop by. We can buy each other a beer."

That caught Joe by surprise. Doesn't this guy know he's talking to a Cheo?

"I'll do that," he said. "Same here. Take care."

217

He sat at his desk. Everything's tied up in a neat little package and ready to be chalked off, he thought. Should he let it go? He could do that. The sad truth was there was no way in hell he could prove Albert's involvement in any of this. Though circumstances , however weak, offer some support for his suspicion. He got up and went home.

~~~

Tiny had just left Albert and felt lucky to be alive. He realized the only reason he was still breathing is that he'd kept to his story. He'd rehearsed it over and over on the trip back to Hilo.

He'd explained why the drugs were no longer in the locker—that the police had taken them—leaving out the part about the baseball bat and the bartender kicking them out of the bar. He'd said that Pepe had fallen overboard and drowned but didn't admit it was an accident. He had let Albert assume that he had pushed him. He'd also taken credit for insisting they take the tugboat when Pepe wanted to fly back, which was actually true, but not because of any murderous plan for getting rid of him.

In truth, he was glad the drugs were no longer around. He'd been afraid that if Albert could've sold them, he might have found himself no longer needed. Albert would have moved on to something new. Now perhaps they could get back to the old life. He'd been much happier then.

Chapter 37

Joe was seated at his desk when Walt Douglas came into the detectives' room. The morning shift had already begun.

"You spend the night?" Walt chuckled, putting his briefcase on his own desk and sitting down.

"Check the sign-in board. My name's the first one on it today."

"Lola must've fainted."

"I also bought the paper. Interesting little article at the bottom of page three."

Joe shoved the newspaper over to Walt.

"Think there's anything to it?" he asked after reading it.

"I think there's a tsunami coming," Joe said. "The other day there were only a couple of churches on Maui against the gambling bill. Now Kauai has got on board with them. By the end of the week, it'll be front-page news. Every church in Hawaii will be up in arms."

"Maybe the whole thing will blow over," Walt shrugged. "Important people have a lot riding on the bill passing."

"Won't matter. It'll be dead on arrival if it even makes it that far."

"Anything else I should know about?"

"One more item but it's not in the paper."

Walt gave him sketchy look.

"Okay," he said. "Let's have it."

"First, what are you working on today?"

"Got another burglary. High-end apartment in a fancy neighborhood. Interview the lady this morning. Why?"

"Like some help?"

"Sure. Ito give you clemency?"

"Better. He's moving to headquarters. Lola told me. Not official yet but it'll be announced soon. So I'm sticking around."

"What about patrol?"

"Lillian and I had a long talk about that. She's fully behind me on whatever I decide but you know what they say."

"Actually, I don't."

"You can't go back."

The End

Thank you for reading. Please review this book. Reviews help others find Absolutely Amazing eBooks and inspire us to keep providing these marvelous tales.

If you would like to be put on our email list to receive updates on new releases, contests, and promotions, please go to AbsolutelyAmazingEbooks.com and sign up.

About the Author

Robert Coburn is originally from Norfolk, Virginia. After high school in Norfolk, he spent three years in the US Army as a helicopter crew chief stationed in Berlin, Germany. He returned home to attend college at Richmond Professional Institute (Now VCU) in Richmond, Virginia, where he earned a Bachelor of Science degree in Advertising. He also met his wife in Richmond while a student there.

Coburn has worked at major advertising agencies in New York and Los Angeles. His ads have won top awards both nationally and internationally. He is an instrument rated commercial pilot and plays saxophone. He and his wife now live in Carmel, California.

For sales, editorial information, subsidiary rights information
or a catalog, please write or phone or e-mail

AbsolutelyAmazingEbooks
Manhanset House
Shelter Island Hts., New York 11965, US
Tel: 212-427-7139
www.BrickTowerPress.com
bricktower@aol.com
www.IngramContent.com

For sales in the UK and Europe please contact our distributor,
Gazelle Book Services
White Cross Mills
Lancaster, LA1 4XS, UK
Tel: (01524) 68765 Fax: (01524) 63232
email: jacky@gazellebooks.co.uk

www.ingramcontent.com/pod-product-compliance
Lightning Source LLC
Chambersburg PA
CBHW060635260626
47161CB00008B/2899